LOOKING FOR CLASS

By Donald Hinchey

Loveland, Colorado

Dedication

To my confirmands
in all their decisions.

Looking for Class

First Printing

Credits
Edited by Michael D. Warden
Cover and book designed by Judy Atwood Bienick
Cover and illustrations by Peg Magovern

Library of Congress Cataloging-in-Publication Data
Hinchey, Donald, 1943-
Looking for class / by Donald Hinchey.
p. cm. — (What would you do? : 6)
Summary: The reader makes choices determining the course of Jeremy's experience at Windy Point High School. Uses a Christian perspective to explore such aspects of school as grades, course load, and extracurricular activities.
ISBN 1-55945-061-4
1. Plot-your-own stories. [1. High schools—Fiction. 2 Schools—Fiction. 3. Christian life—Fiction. 4. Plot-your-own stories.] I. Title. II. Series.
PZ7.H5688Lo 1991
[Fic]—dc20
90-24287
CIP
AC

Printed in the United States of America

Your Road Map

A wise man once said, "Everyone has the right to choose, but you can't choose the consequences of what you choose." That's what Jeremy Kelly discovers when he moves to a new high school, where hard choices are part of his daily routine.

Go with Jeremy as he struggles with choices—about grades, classes, sports, career, relationships, family, church and God. Many decisions will seem obvious at first but may grow into complicated situations. Other decisions seem impossible, but once they're made, they smooth the way for Jeremy's future. Whatever the decision, you plot the course on this road map of Jeremy's journey through high school.

In a way, this book is a road map of your life too. You've probably struggled with many of the same issues Jeremy does:

"Which courses should I take?"

"How do I get others to accept me?"

"Should I cheat to get good grades?"

"What should I do about college?"

Maybe your choices will take you places Jeremy never goes. That's okay. Life isn't a formula. And the decisions you make may have far more options than the ones you're given for each decision in this book. But through the book, you can see how helping others cheat on a test might hurt them more than it helps them. Or you can see how making good grades doesn't always guarantee happiness in the future.

You can read this book many times and never read the same story twice. And each story has its own set of choices and consequences. Here's how it works. Begin reading at the opening page, and continue until you have to make a decision. Then choose how you want the story to continue, and turn to the page indicated. Your choices determine Jeremy's future.

Your choices may help you determine your own future too. Choices fill every hour of your day. Have you ever thought about how you make those decisions? What process do you use? Who helps you? How does God fit into your decision-making process?

So walk with Jeremy through the doors of Windy Point High School—and into a world of wonderful and terrible possibilities. And remember that God is with you to help you make decisions—for Jeremy and for yourself.

Looking for Class

Not bad. Not bad at all.

The poster hanging over Jeremy's bed had actually looked better in Chicago, but it'd do okay in this room, in this new house. The poster was a promotional for the Beatles' final tour. It was a collector's item. Jeremy had all the Beatles albums on cassette. He'd play them full blast into his headphones at night while his family slept. The poster was tattered and worn and hadn't weathered the move well. But it'd still peeve his mother—she never liked the Beatles. And it made the room look, well, lived in.

Still, it wasn't like the old room.

Jeremy and his family had lived in the old house since he was born. Every night since the move, Jeremy had shut his eyes when he lay in bed, listened to the Beatles, and taken an imaginary tour through the old rooms. He could almost feel the greasy wallpaper in his room, smell the sweaty, familiar stink of the high-tops in his old closet and hear the sound of traffic on the city streets. That was one bad house, Jeremy would think to himself.

As much as Jeremy missed his old house, he missed his old friends more.

Ben was short and fat, but tough. Nobody messed with Ben Barrington. And Kenny Pearson, tall with a flat-top and a laugh that would break up the lunchroom. Great with a basketball too. A real magician under the hoops. Oh, how Jeremy missed those guys!

Jeremy and Kenny were going one-on-one in the driveway back in May when Jeremy's father pulled up in the Buick, jumped out and ran in the house like a kid, shouting back to Jeremy, "Big news, Jeremy! Great news! Get in here!"

And that's when his dad told about the promotion and the transfer, and how the family had better get used to living in the suburbs, and how everyone in the family was supposed to fall over themselves in pride and joy. His father worked for a pharmaceutical company—"My dad's a drug pusher" was one of Jeremy's favorite lines—and was given a new territory. "A real promotion!" he proudly told his family.

■

His family was excited about the move, but in all the confusion nobody had asked Jeremy what he thought. No one seemed to understand what it's like to be 15 and told you have to move, Jeremy thought. "Nobody cares what I think," he shouted at his parents that night in July when the house was scooped out and the truck was packed. "Nobody cares."

His mom and dad tried being sensitive and patient, wise and assuring, but finally they pushed him into the back seat of the Buick and began the two-day trip to Denver and a new life.

■

Jeremy Kelly put the last tack in the poster and looked around his squeaky-clean room. Not bad. Not bad.

Tuesday morning after Labor Day, Jeremy was standing in a line that seemed forever in the west cafeteria at Windy Point High School. Registration Day. He felt lonely and awkward, missing Ben and Kenny. It seemed everyone else in the line knew one another. The whir of computers filled the room, and the stack of computer cards in his hand made no sense at all. This place is big, Jeremy thought, although he tried his best to act cool and bored. He'd met some kids in his new church who went to the high school. "One of the biggest in the country!" they'd gush and tell him stories about the classes, the teachers and students—thousands of students.

And the choice of classes! Back in Chicago, one teacher taught three subjects. "Here, it's just like college," the guys from church assured him. "You can take just about anything you can think of."

"Oh, great. Just what I need," Jeremy mumbled. "More decisions."

He looked at the registration material in his hand. Computer forms and cards with spaces to mark with a #2 pencil. As near as he could tell, his schedule broke down into two choices. Either he could take a major load—six classes with world history, algebra, biology, English literature, Spanish, and Earth sciences. Or go the wimpy way—mix up three of the required courses with three easy electives.

Jeremy bit on the #2 pencil and cranked up his Walkman. Part of his brain was saying, "Hey, you deserve a break. You're under a lot of stress, buddy. Take it easy."

And then there was the other voice. "C'mon. Don't be a wimp. Give it your best! Go for the gold!"

Suddenly Jeremy looked up. He was in the front of the line and Alan Richards, a young biology teacher in an open-necked white shirt, was looking up at him.

"And what classes would *you* like?" Alan asked with a smile.

What would *you* do?

If he takes a heavy load, turn to page 115.
If he takes a light load, turn to page 51.

Jeremy would remember the walk to Mr. Wilcox's desk for years. In college he joked about it with fraternity brothers. How the old man broke the silence of the test room with "Mr. Kelly" and all eyes looked to the front and then to him.

How he'd pushed himself out of the chair sure that his cheating had been discovered.

How, when he reached the front of the room, Wilcox motioned for him to lean over, and Jeremy's throat had gone completely shut. He couldn't say a word.

"Mr. Kelly, I've been in this business for years," the old man said, "and I know a mathemetician when I see one. I'd like you to be my student assistant for this next semester. Matter of fact, I'd like you to come in at 2:45 this afternoon to help me begin grading this test. I'm sure you have it down anyway!"

Jeremy couldn't believe his ears. He'd completely fooled the man! And Wilcox was considered one of the toughest at Windy Point. That day would remain in his memory for years, inspiring him.

As student assistant, Jeremy knew where he could find all the algebra tests. Study was no longer necessary, and the grades were great. He even made a little money on the side selling test copies to kids.

With a high grade-point average, Jeremy made it into a good liberal arts college where he quickly learned "the system." His fraternity brothers specialized in parties and doing well though doing nothing. Jeremy's grades were good even if he wasn't learning much. By the time he got his first job following graduation, Jeremy's life was a series of shortcuts and cheating. He'd blindly accepted that to get ahead you have to "just get by," and that might require some less-than-honest efforts.

■

For some reason he was thinking of old-man Wilcox today. The courtroom was hot, and his mind was wandering—like that day in class. The judge looked a little like the old algebra teacher. Jeremy's lawyer and accountant were conferring beside him, and when he looked at them, they both looked away. He honestly didn't believe that the faked tax deductions would be noticed. Besides, everybody did it. It wasn't fair that they should pick on him.

"Mr. Kelly, you may approach the bench." Yes, the judge did look like his old algebra teacher. And yes, he knew the walk to the bench would be familiar.

Only this time, Jeremy suspected the verdict might not be the same.

The End

It had been a month since Jeremy's conversation with Beth. A month of ongoing harassment by his former friends and their new recruits. In the lunchroom, the hallways, as he stood by his locker, Jeremy was considered "fair game" for their sarcasm and abuse.

"Hey, how's the pretty boy?" Chad Swenson yelled out across the lunchroom. Jeremy's friends looked up and then looked at him.

"A lot smarter than you'll ever hope to be, Chad." Jeremy smiled and went back to his lunch.

"That's got to hurt," Sam Anderson said.

"Yeah, sometimes," Jeremy said between bites. "I don't know what kick they get out of picking on someone, but maybe some day they'll grow tired of it. Want an apple, Sam?"

■

Years later, Bob Fisher retired and sold his automotive repair shop to Jeremy. Now Kelly Automotive, the shop had the best reputation in the city for honest, reasonable service.

But there were problems internally. One of Jeremy's employees, Richard Olson, was creating problems for everyone in the shop.

"He's a bitter man, Jeremy," Bill exclaimed. Bill worked under Jeremy as the assistant supervisor. "He puts everyone on edge. I don't see why you keep him around."

"He's a good mechanic," Jeremy said. "He's just had a rough life. All he needs is someone to help him loosen up—someone to work with him."

"Well, count me out, Jeremy," Bill responded. "I can't stand to be around the guy anymore. And I think I speak for the other mechanics too."

Bill walked out, and Jeremy sat at his desk to think. He remembered long ago, when he'd stood by his high school teacher even when others ridiculed him for it.

Jeremy had spent many hours with Richard. They'd talked while working on vintage Chevys and after high-powered games of racquetball. Jeremy had been able to get beyond Richard's bitterness to see his hurt.

Richard had suffered years of loneliness and isolation, beginning when he was 5 and was brutally beaten by his father.

Now Jeremy was trying to show Richard the way to healing. He wanted Richard to develop a relationship with Jesus Christ.

No, Jeremy thought. I can't fire him. It wouldn't be right to turn away now.

Two days later, Jeremy got a call at 3 in the morning.

"Jeremy?"

"Uh, yeah . . . Who is this?" Jeremy was still mostly asleep.

"Jeremy, this is Richard. Sorry to call so late, but I had to tell you something."

Jeremy sat up in bed. He wondered if Richard was in trouble. "Yeah, Rich, that's okay. What's up?"

"Well . . . I almost killed myself tonight, Jeremy. I had the rifle cocked and shoved in my mouth."

"Why, Richard?" Then Jeremy remembered his suicide-prevention training seminar at church. "Where are you, Richard?"

"It's okay, buddy, I'm not going to do it." Richard's voice sounded shaky on the phone. "I couldn't do it—because of you."

"Me? What do you mean?"

"Nobody else has ever stood by me, Jeremy. Nobody. But you do. I know the guys at work have been hassling you to fire me. But you haven't done it."

"That's right, Richard. I haven't."

Richard continued. "While I was sitting here ready to blow off my head, I couldn't quit thinking about all the talks we've had about love and healing—and Jesus. It gave me hope, you know?"

"It's the truth, Richard," Jeremy said. "Jesus can help you start over."

"Yeah, well, I know I'll never get a fresh start on my own." Richard paused. "Jeremy, I think I'm ready to try Jesus. I want to give my life to him—if he wants it."

"Oh, he wants it, Richard." Jeremy smiled as his eyes filled with tears. "He wants it very much. Tell me where you are, and I'll come over."

"Thanks, Jeremy." Richard sounded like he was crying too. "Thanks for sticking by me."

Jeremy smiled and looked toward the ceiling. Thank you, Lord, he prayed silently. Thank you for Richard. And thank you for helping me love him because you do.

Amen.

The End

By the end of the week, Mom and Dad had finally calmed down. But they soon became "education vigilantes," patroling the hall outside Jeremy's room each evening—just to be sure he was studying like he was supposed to.

Jeremy felt like a prisoner in his own home. If the radio went on, if he decided to make a phone call, they'd ask, "Jeremy! Are you doing your homework?" How childish! How suspicious!

Not that they didn't have something to worry about. Jeremy's grades, once so strong when they lived in Chicago, had dipped to an all-time low. Much of his parents' free time was spent in parent-teacher conferences, and it was starting to wear on them.

There were many reasons for the bad grades. Jeremy was having a hard time concentrating, and school wasn't all that interesting. He didn't understand algebra. Teachers didn't seem to have the extra time to help him. Church stuff was more fun. He felt tired most of the time. Listening to his Beatles music was fun and relaxing. All kinds of excuses, but they didn't count with his parents.

"We're prepared to invest a lot of money into your education, Jeremy," Dad would say (over and over), "and we expect you to invest yourself in it as well."

■

It was late afternoon. Jeremy came into the house by the back entrance, quietly closing the door behind him. Maybe they'd forget about the test, he thought. It was a midterm, and Jeremy had been up until midnight preparing for it. And listening to Beatles tunes. But none of his work did much good. Dad was home early from work and there was no cooking smell in the house. That meant they'd be going out for pizza. Great!

"So how'd the exam go, Jeremy?" Dad asked from the dining room table.

"Uh, okay, I guess."

"You guess? Don't you know?" Dad was always on the edge of anger these days. Jeremy decided to face up to his dad and the truth.

"Actually, I do know. It didn't go well. I'm sure I failed."

"Another F!" Dad slammed his fist on the table, bringing his mother in from the hallway.

"Oh, no, Jeremy," Mom said sadly.

Dad gets angry; Mom gets sad. Why is it always the same? Jeremy thought.

Dad was growing red in the face. "We've tried and tried so hard, Jeremy, and this is the best you can do? God has given you more brains than this. Why aren't you using them?"

"Bill, don't get too angry. Jeremy, what's your excuse now? You've had the time. We've tried to take an interest in your work."

"An interest?" Jeremy shouted. "You stand over me like I'm 3 years old! You nag me 'til I can't think for myself anymore. I feel like a criminal for bringing home a paper under a B. And then on Sundays I hear all that talk about forgiveness and love! What a joke!"

Jeremy felt himself starting to cry and immediately felt ashamed.

"It's okay, Jeremy." Mom sat down next to him and put her arm around him. "You're right. We've been hard on you. We've just wanted you to be the best you can be. We just feel you have more potential than we're seeing. But maybe we've not been listening to you enough. If academics aren't a priority for you, what is? What do you want to do?"

Dad calmed down too. "What about the work-study program at Windy Point?" he asked. "It's gotten a lot of publicity lately. The program is doing some creative things."

Jeremy looked at his feet. He wanted to crawl under the table. To be in work-study was a sign you couldn't make it in the regular classroom. Yet the idea did appeal to him. He'd always wanted to learn a trade like auto mechanics or something.

"I'll think about it," he said softly. "I guess I'll go to my room. Why don't you guys go out without me?"

What would *you* do?

If Jeremy stays in the academic program, turn to page 84.
If he chooses work-study, turn to page 61.

Jeremy could hear birds chirping in the semidarkness and knew his study time was drawing to a close. It'd been a long night, but the history exam was now just two hours away, and there really was no other choice. His hamstrings still ached from the workout the day before. That had helped him stay awake all night.

Actually, he really didn't feel too bad. His eyes burned, his head ached and his muscles were sore, but he was still functioning. Facts rumbled around in his head, but they all ran together—Columbus, Queen Isabella, Miles Standish and Martin Luther—what team did they play for? He laughed and hoped that when the questions were asked, all the dates and names would fit together.

The team had been doing great! It was on its way to the semifinals, and Jeremy had played five minutes in the third quarter with Windy Point out ahead 20 points. His jump shot swished in over the head of Cherry Creek's guard, and the crowd cheered wildly.

But then, reality. A history final and no study time. A paper due in biology. The Bible study at church he'd promised to lead. Soon, it was 10 p.m. and there was only one choice—the dreaded all-nighter.

■

The exam didn't go well. Jeremy couldn't even remember why Columbus had sailed for the new world. Martin Luther was German, but he couldn't remember much more. His eyes grew heavy in the warm room, and soon his head was on his desk. Mr. Mullins shook Jeremy's shoulder to wake him. What's more, basketball practice that afternoon was a joke. The coach sent him home.

■

Report cards were mailed home at Windy Point, and the torn envelope was on the dining room table when Jeremy walked in from basketball practice that next Wednesday. He could tell from the silence in the house that all was not well.

"Jeremy, could you come here, please?"

His father's voice was hard. It wasn't really a request.

The computer print-out was on the kitchen table facing him.

His dad was still in his lab coat. Mom, a greasy apron over her dress, stood at the stove.

One A, three B's, a C, and an F—in world history. That final exam did it. He should've stayed awake!

Dad sat at the table. "We've talked to you about your schedule, supported you and tried to help you, Jeremy. But something's got to change. Your mother and I know you can do better than this!"

Dad's hardness surprised him. Mom only stood and stared. The computer paper in his hand was a mocking reminder of his failure.

Something was going to have to change.

Blind choice:

Without looking ahead, turn to page 12 or page 94 to see what happens.

Thirty votes. That's all he needed—just thirty votes. If every kid who felt sick on election day had chosen to come to school and vote for him, Jeremy Kelly would be the new student council president.

But they didn't. And he wasn't. And he felt terrible.

Jeremy tried to convince himself that he hadn't wanted to win. That it was a dumb idea in the first place. It was Jeremy's way of coping.

The "victory party" his youth group had promised was bittersweet. Trish, Andrea, Craig Morris, Mark Sims and lots of others got together on Friday night at Trish's home to offer their sympathies. They all wore black, and Jeremy thought it was cute.

Beth arrived and saw everyone's clothes. "Did somebody die?" she asked.

"Jeremy lost," Mark said. "We're comforting him."

"And how does Jeremy feel about that?" Beth asked.

"Actually, I don't feel all that bad," Jeremy said. "I never thought I'd make a good politician."

Beth put her bag down on the sofa and took a deep drink from Trish's Diet Coke. "So what now, Jeremy?" she asked.

Jeremy leaned back. "I guess we all go back to putting up with life as it is at Windy Point," he said.

"Maybe there's a better way," Beth said. "Any ideas?"

Craig piped in. "How about a Bible study at school?"

The kids laughed.

"As if they'll let us."

"As if anyone will come."

"As if anyone will lead us."

"How about the almost-president?" Mark asked. "Maybe Jeremy could be our Bible study leader."

"I think I'm busy feeling sorry for myself because I didn't win the election," Jeremy said. "Find another leader. Maybe they'd let Beth in to teach a class."

"You'd stand a better chance, Jeremy." Beth smiled. "How about it?"

Jeremy breathed a heavy sigh.

What would *you* do?

If he starts the Bible study, turn to page 110.
If he doesn't start the Bible study, turn to page 65.

"It *is* unfair!"

"That's not the issue, Jeremy." Mr. Johnson's voice had lost its sympathy after 10 minutes of heated discussion. He was growing more angry by the second.

"Look, Jeremy, you can feel any way you want about drugs and mandatory testing, but the issue here is whether you or any student can print an editorial that contradicts Parents Council policy!"

Jeremy sat down and sighed.

"Mr. Johnson, I hate drugs and what they do to kids. But mandatory testing isn't the way to fight them, and I think I have a right to say that in print—whether it contradicts Parents Council policy or not! That's part of free press."

Jeremy leaned back in his chair and listened to the silence in the room. Then he spoke.

"Okay, you have the authority, and I don't. I won't fight you on this even though I think you're wrong. You've been at Windy Point a few more years than I have, and you'll be here after I'm gone. But couldn't we have something that tells us what we can and can't publish—like a guideline or something? That way no one has to go through this again."

Mr. Johnson was perplexed by Jeremy. One minute Jeremy was a child throwing a tantrum, the next, a young adult wanting to negotiate.

"Jeremy, you're a real puzzle," Mr. Johnson laughed as he reached for his legal pad.

■

Jeremy was late for his world history class, so he ran down the east wing to the stairwell and up to the second door on the right. He was breathing hard as he put the assistant principal's note on Mr. Mullins' desk and took his seat near the window. Mullins stopped his lecture, looked Jeremy over and waited until Jeremy was seated before continuing.

It was a warm day with sunlight spilling in over the desks. Jeremy could see that half the class was asleep. But Mr. Mullins continued his lecture on medieval politics in apparent oblivion.

"The German nobility wanted to break from the Roman Papacy at any cost, and a young monk named Martin Luther made this possible."

Jeremy's attention picked up. They had studied the Protestant Reformation in Sunday school. His youth minister, Beth Faulkes, had even shown a video that made Luther seem like a human and not just a historical character.

"Whereas some reflect on the Reformation as a zealous religious revival, historical fact would, in fact, dictate otherwise," Mullins droned.

Why can't this guy speak normal English? Jeremy thought. Guess he wants to impress us.

"In the minds of the nobles," Mullins said, "the real goal of the Protestant Reformation was to separate from the Catholic church. And they used Martin Luther to accomplish their goal."

"Mr. Mullins?"

Jeremy sat up straight in his chair and spoke loud enough for all the class to hear. Even the sleepers looked up.

"I thought the reason Martin Luther broke from the Roman Catholic church was that he disagreed with its religious beliefs," Jeremy said. "He disagreed with the church's position on how people get eternal life—whether by God's grace or through works."

Mr. Mullins stared blankly at Jeremy. "That theory has been popularized by the church for hundreds of years. But that doesn't apply to our discussion here."

"Why not? I mean, we've talked about the Reformation in my church before, and the information I got there . . ."

"Part of education, Jeremy," Mullins interrupted, "is realizing that everything we hear in Sunday school isn't always true. Now please let me continue."

Jeremy was confused. Why wouldn't Mr. Mullins hear what he had to say? Could what Jeremy heard at church be wrong? Jeremy wanted to get advice from someone at the church, then talk about it with Mr. Mullins again. But part of him wanted to just drop the issue. After all, hadn't he been a champion for enough causes today already?

What would *you* do?

If Jeremy gets advice and continues the argument, turn to page 82.

If he blows it off, turn to page 59.

"I thought I could make a difference here, Dad," Jeremy said softly. He was sitting at the kitchen table toying with a glass of milk. "Except the school has absolute control over what's written, and what I was writing isn't acceptable."

"I hear what you're saying, Son," Dad said sympathetically. "Mr. Johnson would be responsible to his authorities for your editorial, and apparently he didn't agree with it, or he didn't want to be responsible for having to defend you."

"So what should I do?" Jeremy asked. "If I stay on the newspaper staff I'll be compromising my position; but if I quit, it's kind of like giving up. It's like I can't make a good choice."

"Yeah, I run into that a lot," Dad said. "There are some choices where nobody wins and everybody has to be content with the result. What do you feel you've got to do?"

"I've got to quit, Dad. To prove a point, but also because I can't fight Mr. Johnson."

■

Jeremy's resignation letter went from four pages to two pages to three sentences. He'd thought of just writing "I Quit!" on a large banner, but that seemed too dramatic. His final note was to the point and brief:

Dear Mr. Johnson,

Due to the censoring of my last article to the school paper, I've decided I can no longer be a part of the Windy Point editorial staff. I'm therefore submitting my resignation. I hope I can find other ways to help our school become a better place for us all.

Mr. Johnson read the note and put the paper on his desk.

"Thanks, Jeremy," he said. "I'm sorry to have to accept this, but I understand. So what do you want to do to help our school 'become a better place for us all'?"

"I'm not sure. One idea I have is for a Bible study at school."

"At school? You mean, in the building?"

"Yes. Our Bible studies at church are really great. Lots of kids come and we discuss some pretty heavy issues. I think something like that could make a real difference at Windy Point."

Jeremy was excited. Mr. Johnson was worried.

"Jeremy, you're young and idealistic." Mr. Johnson was

sounding like someone's TV father. "If you were to try to start this Bible study, I don't know if it would really work. Not in this environment."

"You could be right, Mr. Johnson. Maybe it would never fly. But what if you're wrong? It could be really neat."

"Just think about what I've said, Jeremy," Mr. Johnson replied.

"Okay, Mr. Johnson," Jeremy sighed. "I'll think about it."

What would *you* do?

If Jeremy starts a Bible study, turn to page 110.
If he forgets about the Bible study, turn to page 65.

Jeremy stopped by Fisher Automotive on his way home from school. He was feeling great. The SAT scores were in, and Jeremy had done well. He had to tell someone, and Bob Fisher had taken a real interest in Jeremy over the past two weeks.

Although Jeremy had opted not to join the work-study program, Bob had offered him a weekend job. Jeremy almost immediately admired the gentle man for welcoming him—an auto novice—so readily into his garage.

When Jeremy told Bob the good news, Mr. Fisher congratulated him and threw him a soft drink from a small refrigerator in the back room.

"Wish I was as happy as you are, Jeremy," Mr. Fisher said, taking a long gulp from his soft drink. "I've been in this business 18 years, and finding good help is my biggest pain. Just had to let another guy go on Friday. He just couldn't figure out which end of the screwdriver to use."

Jeremy laughed sympathetically.

"It's their loss, Bob," Jeremy said. "Anyone who works for you gets an education as well as a job. I'd give anything to work here full time."

"When can you start?"

Jeremy was stunned. Bob Fisher had offered him a job! They worked out the details: eight hours a day starting in the summer doing apprentice work under Bob's supervision. An hourly wage that was twice what kids made at the fast-food places. And if Jeremy could work overtime, Mr. Fisher would pay time and a half. What a break!

Jeremy was still excited Thursday when he walked into his appointment with Mr. Campbell.

"Those SAT scores are good, Jeremy," Mr Campbell grinned, "and I'll bet with a little extra work on your courses, most colleges would jump to have you!" Jeremy smiled.

"What kind of extra work?"

"Looking at your transcript, I'm seeing some weakness in math and science, Jeremy." Mr. Campbell was writing Jeremy's hours on a yellow legal pad on his desk. He pulled out a paperback catalog. "Most schools require advanced math and science work, and you don't presently have any. It's not a real problem, though."

"Oh, I can take them next year?"

"No, not really. You're going to be pushing hard just to get your required courses in. Summer school is the only way."

"Summer school?" Jeremy slumped deep in his seat.

"Yes. Summer school begins at George Washington High on June 6 and runs through August 22. You could take Spanish and advanced chemistry in the morning, and geometry in the afternoon. It's pretty heavy, but you could handle it. That would easily bring your transcript up to the toughest college entrance standards. What do you say?"

Jeremy leaned forward in his chair and told Mr. Campbell about the job. He explained that Bob Fisher was one of the best mechanics in the city, and the pay was incredible. And if he did well, he'd have permanent work without college.

"But how do you know auto mechanics is what you want?" Mr. Campbell asked.

"I don't," Jeremy admitted. "That's why I need to work at it this summer. I figure I still have time before college to get prepared if I don't like what I'm doing at the shop."

"That is, if you don't want to get into a top-notch college," his adviser interrupted. "Look, Jeremy, your grades are good, but the best colleges are very competitive. With these three courses on your transcript, you stand a good chance of getting in. Without them . . . who knows?"

He handed Jeremy the summer-school catalog and got out of his chair. "Let me know by Monday, okay? Deadline for enrollment is Tuesday."

On the walk home, Jeremy paused in front of Fisher Automotive. The smell of the place was sweet to him. Bob looked up from under a car and waved and smiled. Jeremy smiled back and kept on walking. A summer-school classroom would never smell as sweet!

What would *you* do?

If Jeremy goes to summer school, turn to page 57.
If he takes the job, turn to page 118.

Alan Richards motioned for the guys to come closer so he could whisper. Jeremy felt fresh beads of sweat forming on his face.

"I wanted to let you guys know I really appreciate your work this semester."

"Huh?" Jeremy said. Chris smiled.

"Obviously I haven't seen your test scores yet, but you guys have been two of the hardest workers in this class all semester long. Jeremy, I especially want to thank you for helping Chris learn the material. Ever since you asked to work together, I've been thinking about how good it is to see kids who're willing to go the extra mile for each other."

Jeremy couldn't believe his ears. Not only had he and Chris gotten away with cheating on the exam, they were being congratulated by their teacher! Jeremy had overestimated this man. He was really a pushover!

"Well, thanks, Mr. Richards," Chris started to say, but when he saw Jeremy's look, he quickly shut up.

"It's easy to work hard when we've got a good teacher like you, Mr. Richards," Jeremy said, trying to sound sincere. "Thanks for your confidence."

"Well, Jeremy, I'd like to talk with you about being my student assistant. I could use someone to help me grade papers, and I think you're just the man. What do you say?"

"I'd be honored, Mr. Richards," Jeremy said with a smile. "I'd really like that."

Back at the locker, Chris and Jeremy laughed loud and "high-fived" each other.

"Do you believe that, Kelly?" Chris asked, his eyes wide. "I don't believe you! You're a genius!"

Jeremy had to admit he'd really fooled Mr. Richards. And it wasn't as though he'd done anything wrong. Jeremy really tried to believe that. He had a friend who needed help, and he helped him. Isn't that what friends are for?

As the weeks went by, Jeremy found others who were having difficulty in Mr. Richards' science courses. He also found Mr. Richards' file drawer of quizzes, and it wasn't long before test questions were being photocopied and slipped to kids after school. At $5 a quiz, Jeremy was making good money "helping his friends."

It was risky, of course. He would go to Mr. Richards' office at 2 after his last class and copy the quizzes before the teacher got back at 3. But he made it work.

Coming into the office one Tuesday, Jeremy checked the hallway to make sure nobody was around and quietly lifted the coming week's worth of quizzes from Mr. Richards' file. Then he walked to the machine, lifted the cover and placed the first quiz on the glass.

He pressed the "copy" button and looked over his shoulder to find Mr. Richards standing behind him.

"You want to tell me what you're doing, Jeremy?"

"What are you doing here? You're supposed to be in class."

"I came back for my lab coat. What are *you* doing?" the biology teacher's voice was strained and harsh.

"Well, uh, I'm just helping you by copying some of these quizzes for you. I figured you might lose this file, and . . ."

"That's a lie! You're passing out quizzes to your friends, aren't you, Jeremy?"

Mr. Richards looked like he might blow up. He said, "I trusted you, and you used me. We've got a trip to take, fella'! Let's pay a visit to the principal."

Blind choice:

Without looking ahead, turn to page 102 or page 119 to see what happens to Jeremy.

The next morning he was in the south parking lot at 8, when Matt and Justin pulled up in Justin's old Jeep. It was caked with mud and there wasn't an inch that wasn't dented or rusted. A beer can rolled out from under the seat as they roared out of the parking lot headed west.

About 5 miles out of town Justin veered off on County Road 33 south to "The Greens." Jeremy had heard about the place. Rolling, steep hills with years' worth of tire tracks gouging the sides. Jeremy thought about the kids sitting in a boring classroom, and he felt good and crazy.

For the next few hours they screamed up and down slopes, yelling until they were hoarse. Around noon, they drove back into town for lunch at a fast-food place. They talked for a long time, reliving the thrills of the morning.

"Man, am I wired!" Matt shouted as they drove Jeremy home.

"Yeah, that was great," Jeremy agreed. "It sure beat a day in class!"

They were passing the school when Justin had a brainstorm.

"Look," he said suddenly, pointing to the construction field north of the gymnasium.

"See that bulldozer?" Matt and Jeremy nodded. "I heard they don't take the keys at night. Just leave 'em under the seat." He pulled the Jeep over by the field, and the three of them looked at the big yellow machine.

"How'd it be if that monster found its way into the teachers' lot by tomorrow morning?" Matt and Justin howled at the thought. Jeremy was quiet.

"What d'ya say, guys?" Justin asked. His eyes were glowing.

"Count me in," said Matt. "I'll bet I can run that puppy."

"What about you, Jeremy?" The two looked at him. "Want to do a little earth-moving tonight? We'll meet here around 10."

Jeremy leaned against the back of the seat and looked away. Now, that would be a challenge!

What would *you* do?

If Jeremy goes along with the prank, turn to page 38.
If he refuses to go along, turn to page 78.

Chris was waiting at Jeremy's locker at 7:45 with the look of a little kid pestering his parents.

"Well, you gonna do it?" Chris leaned forward as Jeremy opened the locker door.

Jeremy looked down at his books. "Yeah. I guess so."

Chris let out a whoop. "I knew I could count on you! You won't regret this, Kelly. This is the last time. The very last time. After this, I'm on my own. I promise."

They discussed how Jeremy would place the exam on his desk and position his body so he'd page Mr. Richards' view of Chris. If Mr. Richards got up, Jeremy would move his paper back into the center and wait until it was safe before moving it back again. They talked about changing some sentences and misspelling a few words so Mr. Richards wouldn't notice the similarities in their answers.

Jeremy felt sick. It wasn't just the heat in the room. It was him. He really liked Mr. Richards, and he knew it was wrong to cheat. But he'd let Chris cheat before. Now, it seemed only right that he should protect him ... just one more time.

At 8:01 Mr. Richards passed out the tests, gave instructions and called for silence. Sweat dotted Jeremy's forehead. He moved the paper to the right and shifted his body so Chris was covered. He felt Chris move close to his right shoulder.

It all went smoothly. By 8:50 the test was done, and Jeremy felt confident he'd done well. Both guys turned in their papers ... several minutes apart. Jeremy hoped Chris had remembered to change a few answers.

As he returned to his seat, Jeremy shot a glance at Chris behind him. Chris was grinning from ear to ear. Jeremy rolled his eyes.

"Jeremy. Chris. Could you come up here for a minute?"

The two boys looked at each other in shock. They gathered up their books and started for the front of the room.

Mr. Richards stood up as they approached the desk. He was holding their test papers in his right hand. The teacher cleared his throat.

Blind choice:

Without looking ahead, turn to page 23 or page 125 to see whether Jeremy and Chris are caught cheating.

The next six weeks hadn't been easy for Jeremy. After school let out at 3, he'd catch the bus home, shoot some hoops and then hit the books.

Mom would get home from work by 5:15. They'd have dinner, and Jeremy was back studying by 6:30. Sometimes it was 11 or later before he'd get to bed—to be up by 5:30 the next morning. It was hard, and he missed sports and other activities. But it was worth it. His test scores were coming in at 95 and higher, and classmates were noticing.

He had to admit that the reason for taking the heavy load of classes was these kids. They were such snobs! At his old school he knew all the kids. They'd all grown up going to the same schools, and grades were no big deal. But here in the suburbs, everyone was new. And the competition was incredible! Jeremy wasn't about to be outdone by anyone.

Jeremy worked hard to earn everyone's respect, and soon he became known as the "Chicago brain." He liked that a lot.

Jeremy's lab partner, Chris Miller, was also popular. But it wasn't because of his grades. In fact, Chris wasn't doing well at all in biology. He was a smooth-talking guy with a nice Mustang and a lot of money. He won his popularity by giving people gifts in return for favors.

"Jeremy, I've got this problem," Chris said as they walked down the hall one day. "This biology project is really bugging me." The project counted for one-fourth of the final grade. "I need help," Chris said.

Jeremy stopped. "What do you mean?" he asked.

Chris grinned. "Here's my idea: We'll tell Richards we want to double up on the project. You know, we'll do the research together, and it'll be twice as big as a regular project."

"That's a neat idea, Chris," Jeremy said, seeing an opportunity to make a friend. "I can help you catch up on some of the work too."

"No, you don't understand, buddy," Chris said with a smile. "I'll let *you* do the work. I don't understand this stuff anyway, and you're good. You can do this stuff in your sleep. I just want half the credit."

"Sounds like a one-sided deal to me," Jeremy said, not sure whether Chris was serious.

"I'll make it worth your while, Jeremy. Just name your price.

You want to use my Mustang for the homecoming dance? It's yours. You need some money? Maybe a hundred bucks would persuade you."

Jeremy stood silent for a second. Then he said, "I'll have to let you know tomorrow, Chris. Okay?"

"Yeah, sure," Chris chuckled. "Tomorrow."

It's going to be a long night, Jeremy thought, as he walked to his next class.

What would *you* do?

If he does the project for Chris, turn to page 66.
If he refuses to share the project, turn to page 47.

Jeremy changed his courses the next day. It wasn't the "genius track," he explained to his parents, but it was still enough to keep him busy. The history course was changed to world history. And biology and algebra were added. Health and fitness stayed—but then, so did basketball.

Each day, Jeremy came in exhausted after two hours of drills on the courts, had dinner, watched a half-hour of television and then hit the books.

And then there was church. Back in Chicago, the Kellys had been active in their congregation. Dad on Council, Mom in congregational ministry. Jeremy liked Sunday school, and youth group was important. He'd even been planning to go to a national youth conference.

The church in Denver was great too. Jeremy liked the youth minister. Beth Faulkes was young and single, loved camping and hiking, and could relate well with the kids. He even heard rumors she had her pilot's license and took kids on campouts in remote wilderness areas.

Jeremy was getting to know the youth group, and the kids were already looking up to him. Mom and Dad had warned about getting "too involved" first semester. "You've got exams coming," they said.

Jeremy studied but not like he should've. Too much going on, just like in Chicago. School's important, Jeremy figured, but so's church. And there's always basketball too.

But as midterm exams approached, all the facts, all the concepts and books were getting mixed up in his head. He tried to study different subjects on different nights; still history, algebra, biology and even basketball plays seemed to run together.

He entered the classroom on test days with a blur of facts, statistics and confusion running between his ears. Later when his parents asked how he did, he nodded "okay," but he really wasn't sure.

Blind choice:

Without looking ahead, turn to page 68 or page 129 to see how he did.

"Six weeks! It's taken them six weeks to decide on a dumb college application? You'd think I was asking for a million dollars or something!"

Every day when he'd get home from school, Jeremy would check the mailbox, looking for the Gundermann College seal on the envelopes. As the days passed, he grew more worried, especially as others in his class came in each day with news of their acceptance.

He'd applied to Gundermann for many reasons, the main one being that it had everything he wanted: a small student body, top-notch professors and a beautiful campus.

But his grades were the problem. In spite of a great summer-school experience, Jeremy's grades just barely qualified him for Gundermann.

■

The envelope was on the table when he got home from school on Friday. He opened it carefully, holding it as if it were fragile.

"Dear Mr. Kelly, we regret to inform you that your application for admission . . . " He didn't have to finish it. He saw something about GPA, and he knew his efforts were too late. Jeremy felt ashamed, like he'd let God, himself and his family down.

"You must be disappointed, Son," Dad said after hearing the news.

"Yeah."

"You want to talk about it?"

Jeremy just played with the envelope between his fingers.

"Do you think you've disappointed us?"

"I guess."

Dad sat in the chair next to Jeremy and looked at the letter. "What matters most to me, Jeremy," he said, "is that you're happy and fulfilled. God has given you a lot of gifts and there are lots of places you can develop them. Gundermann College is only one."

"But I'll be so embarrassed on Monday. All the other kids have been accepted at major schools."

"Jeremy," Dad said seriously, "it's not a rule of life that all kids must go to college right out of high school. And it doesn't follow that kids who go to college will be immediate successes while kids who choose other paths will fail. It's how hard you work to develop the talents God gives you. I think it's time we get creative about your future. There are plenty of options out there."

"Yeah. Maybe on Monday we can go to Metropolitan Community College," Jeremy seemed to brighten. "A couple of my friends say it has a good program. And maybe after a year or two, I could reapply to Gundermann."

"Or maybe not," Dad said. "Let's be open to what God has in store for you, Jeremy. I have a feeling we'll all be surprised!"

Jeremy crushed the letter into a tight ball and arched it into the trash can. The world for him was still filled with choices.

The End

The half-hour in Janet Gill's office would be long remembered.

Chris Miller made sure the word got out about "sweet Jeremy Kelly" and the way he charmed the principal. Matt Brondos and Justin Parsons were waiting by the convenience store as he walked by that afternoon, and Jeremy soon found himself with a new group of friends—a group convinced that Jeremy could talk his way out of anything.

The next two years at Windy Point were good for Jeremy. He found a group of seniors who sold math and biology tests, and he bought the business from them. It made good money and helped him with his grades. His English papers were written by a college sophomore, and history exams were always A's and B's—thanks to willing friends and an ingenious system of sharing answers.

His folks were proud of him on graduation day, and Jeremy felt just a bit guilty. "If only they knew what I don't know ..." he joked to Chris.

College went pretty much the same. "It's a game," Jeremy would tell his friends. "Learn the system and succeed."

And that he did. With an impressive grade-point average and a smooth line of talk, Jeremy graduated with a long line of job interviews and his choice of high-paid positions.

He was thinking about all of that as he sat in his apartment flipping through the want ads. The first job had lasted a month before they figured out he was all talk. The second and third jobs lasted a little longer. He'd learned "the system" by then and could bluff better. But finally, the supervisors wanted results, not excuses.

And so Jeremy sat scanning the want ads on a November Monday morning with a TV game show playing mindlessly in the background.

"It just isn't fair," he muttered to himself. "Life just isn't fair. I'm trying hard, but nobody seems to care. They should be giving me a break. Like my college profs and high school teachers. Mrs. Gill gave me a break."

And for the first time, Jeremy wondered if his old high school principal had really helped him.

The End

"You know, Jeremy, I don't know ..." Craig's voice trailed off as he swept the floor of Room 224.

"Don't know what, Craig?"

"I don't know if this Bible study business is such a good idea. Don't get me wrong, I like the Bible and all that, but ..."

"What he's trying to say is you've got yourself a real bunch of snobs here, Jeremy," Trish interrupted.

The Bible study had started out great, and the large crowds came for a month until some kids began to insist that their way of interpreting the Bible was the only right way. Jeremy tried to keep them on the subject, but they became angry and left.

The Bible study group was down to around 15 when the smoking argument began. It started over ashtrays on restaurant tables, which some claimed only encouraged smoking. The two guys in the group who smoked said it was their business and nobody else's.

Soon people were leaving left and right.

■

"It seemed like such a good idea, Beth," Jeremy told his youth minister after Sunday school. "I thought we'd all get together and read the Bible and pray and maybe sing some songs, and it started out great."

"So what happened?" Beth asked.

"They all started arguing and bad-mouthing one another. And we started fighting over issues. It just took over."

"So how are you feeling about your Bible study?"

"Sometimes I don't want to go anymore. It's no fun. The 10 kids who still come just sit around and congratulate each other on how religious we are and what a mess the rest of the students have become."

"That's human nature, Jeremy." Beth sat on the edge of her desk. "People always want to make themselves look good. It's called sin, and if we could fight it ourselves, Jesus would've been a cheerleader and not gotten himself crucified."

"So you're saying I should disband the Bible study?"

"I'm saying you should do whatever God leads you to do."

Jeremy hated it when she did that. It would be easier for him to take some advice. Why did she always leave him to make the decision alone?

■

After much prayer, Jeremy decided he'd continue the Bible study. Maybe other kids would join it. Maybe things could change through prayer.

It sure is lonely being right, though, Jeremy thought as he left for school one morning later that year. But that, too, is part of being like Jesus.

Jesus didn't always have popular opinion on his side either.

The End

Craig, Trish and Jeremy were cleaning up the room after the crowd left that morning.

"You'd better get yourself to class, Jeremy, or we'll have to pray for you to repent!" Trish laughed as she picked up the last few wadded papers.

"That's the first time I've heard a prayer in this room, I think," Craig said softly. "Maybe it'll help my grades in this class."

"Maybe, Craig," Jeremy laughed. "But either way, it was a good Bible study. All the kids seemed interested."

Trish looked at Jeremy. "It helped to have them form small groups, Jeremy. I heard some of them talking, and they were pretty involved."

"Let's hope it makes a difference," Jeremy sighed.

■

It's hard to notice when an attitude changes, but something began to be different at Windy Point. The kids who attended the Bible study each week told other kids about it, and soon Room 224 was packed with students reading, talking and praying.

Teachers noticed too. Kids seemed less apathetic about school. A bunch of them even stopped wearing their purposely offensive T-shirts.

■

"Kelly, I got a letter about you. I think you should read it." Mr. Johnson stopped Jeremy on his way to class.

Jeremy took the letter from Mr. Johnson's hand and leaned up against a locker. What had he done now? he wondered.

"Dear Mr. Johnson," the letter began. It was from Carl Newton!

"I left Windy Point because the rumors about homosexuality were making it impossible for me to teach. That was the most painful thing I've ever had to do in my life, as you might imagine." Jeremy felt a catch in his throat. He continued.

"Since then I've enrolled in a masters' degree program and have even started work on my first book. It looks like things are working out great. Melanie and I will be married this August.

"I want to let you know I've heard through some of my friends about Jeremy Kelly's new Bible study. They've noticed the difference it's made among the students, but probably few teachers will say anything to Jeremy. Please let him know he's doing a great job in bringing good from what was an evil situation. That's what Jesus did, and that's what he wants his followers to do.

"Send me Jeremy's address, please, so I can write him personally." The letter was signed, "God bless you. Carl Newton."

Jeremy handed the letter back to Mr. Johnson. Jeremy was speechless.

"Carl's right, Jeremy. You've made a real difference at Windy Point, and we're grateful to you. Keep up the good work."

As Mr. Johnson walked away, Jeremy realized how hard it was for the assistant principal to admit that a Bible study could be all that great. Jeremy felt honored and amazed at the same time.

God's surprises are too much! he thought to himself as he closed the locker. Just too much!

The End

Jeremy had yawned throughout the evening. And finally, at 9:30 he announced it was bedtime for him. His parents looked at him like he was crazy, but Mom said something about how the rest would do him good and kissed him goodnight. By 9:45, he'd slipped out his window and was running through the neighbor's back yard to the street.

Justin and Matt were waiting by the dumpster in the school parking lot. The bulldozer sat about 100 yards away, looking like a prehistoric monster in the moonlight.

The guys spoke in loud whispers as Jeremy approached.

"Hey, I knew you wouldn't let us down." Justin grabbed Jeremy's shoulder and pulled him low by the dumpster.

"The security guard just made his rounds so he should be on the other side of the building," Matt said. "Let's go!"

The three of them made a low, hunching run for the bulldozer, and stopped in its nighttime shadow.

Justin was laughing. "Now, who knows how to drive this monster?"

The two boys looked at him in disbelief.

"I thought you did," Jeremy said. "It was your idea."

"No, I was just kidding before. I don't know the first thing about moving this bucket. Some of us are executives; some of us are workers. How about you, Matt?"

The two looked at Matt.

"No way, man," Matt shook his head. "Jeremy looks much more like the bulldozer type to me."

Jeremy spoke before he had a chance to think. "Okay, okay," he said. "But this means I get all the glory."

Jeremy found the key, pulled himself up into the driver's seat, put the key into the ignition and turned it. He hesitated for a moment, then turned it farther. The engine let out such a roar that he nearly fell off the seat.

"Aim for the parking lot! Take it to the parking lot!" Justin and Matt ran ahead of Jeremy toward the faculty parking lot. Jeremy fumbled with the transmission lever, until suddenly the machine began to lumber forward.

But it was turning! In a slow half-circle the bulldozer pivoted away from the parking lot and moved toward the field house some 30 yards away.

Matt and Justin started running after Jeremy, shouting and

waving their arms. The door to the coach's office was barely 15 yards off.

"The key!" Justin yelled. "Hit the key!"

But in the dark and confusion, Jeremy couldn't find the key. The door was 5 yards in front of him, and Jeremy knew it was time to abandon ship. He jumped to the side, and felt a sharp pain shoot up his leg. As he lay there, he heard the bulldozer plow right into the field house. The scoop jammed into the building's foundation and stalled.

Before long, police sirens filled the night air, and red lights flashed around him. Jeremy tried to run, but the pain in his leg was terrible. Jeremy stopped and watched Justin and Matt being chased down by police officers. Jeremy felt embarrassed. He felt cold, hurt and very much alone.

Within minutes, Jeremy's mom and dad were there, talking to Mrs. Gill, the principal. The whole episode seemed like a blur.

Finally, Mrs. Gill walked over to Jeremy. Jeremy stood up. His leg was beginning to feel better now.

"We'll wait until tomorrow to deal with this matter, Jeremy," the principal said.

Jeremy's parents took him home. And no one said a word.

■

"Right now I see only two alternatives." Mrs. Gill cleared her throat. Jeremy's parents were looking down, silent.

"I can either put you on detention, and get you into some counseling . . . "

Counseling?! What do they think—I'm crazy? Jeremy remained silent.

"Or I can suspend you."

Jeremy's heart sank. "It's very serious, Jeremy." Mrs. Gill was looking straight through him. "I'll let you know my decision in a few hours."

How dumb could I be? Jeremy thought. What a nightmare!

Blind choice:

Without looking ahead, turn to page 102 or page 119 to see what happens to Jeremy.

"Alllrrright!!"

Jeremy was so hyper he felt like climbing the walls. The vote was close but clear. He knew he should be humble, and he tried. But late at night he confided to his dad, "I love it! I just love it! The phone calls, the congratulations—especially the one from Pastor Hughes."

Dad smiled. "Pretty soon the congratulations will stop, though, and you'll have to start fulfilling those campaign promises. That's the hard part of being elected to office."

Jeremy got quiet. "The people who elected me must've thought what I said was important."

Reality had set in. Jeremy Kelly had a lot of work to do!

■

To be president, Jeremy found, he had to go to lots of meetings. Meetings before and after school; meetings during study hall; meetings with the principal, the student council, and with whatever group of students wanted to meet with him.

At the end of his first month, Jeremy was worried. He was going to all the meetings, but hadn't had a chance to work on his campaign promises. When he mentioned textbook review to Mrs. Gill, she smiled and said it was a nice idea. She'd mention it to the academic council at the next meeting.

"Would you like to come to the meeting, Jeremy?" she asked. Jeremy gulped. Another meeting.

"I haven't had a chance to read the novel for Monday's English test, and my algebra work is a joke," Jeremy told his parents after dinner one Friday night. Mom and Dad looked at each other knowingly.

"Then there's the church car wash all day tomorrow and the youth pizza party at Robin Feister's tomorrow night. I've got to go to church Sunday morning and youth Bible study Sunday night. That leaves Sunday afternoon to read 250 pages."

Mom and Dad listened, then quietly continued their meal. They realized Jeremy would have to work this one out on his own.

■

Jeremy somehow made it through the novel, but things just kept getting more hectic.

Sam and Tyra were sympathetic but too busy with their own schedules to help much.

"I got into this because I wanted to make a difference around here," Jeremy complained. "The only difference it's made is I'm real strung out. And nobody seems to care."

"Kids don't care about classroom work," Sam said with a yawn. "What's real important to them is that business about being able to go off campus for lunch. Now, there's a subject we can all sink our teeth into."

The three of them groaned.

Tyra leaned forward. "Sam may be right, Jeremy," she said. "It sounded good to talk about making lots of changes in school, but kids don't want to work for them. I think you're on your own."

On his own. That was the worst feeling of all. Friends could sympathize, parents could support, but Jeremy felt all alone in trying to do what he said he was going to do. And meanwhile, his grades were sliding, and he was neglecting the church activities he knew were important.

For the next few weeks, Jeremy did his best to juggle all his responsibilities and interests. He invested in a Day-Timer and marked it up with colored pens—each color representing a different area of his life. School. Student council. Church. Family. Friends. Every day looked like a bowl of multicolor spaghetti.

But then it happened. Jeremy walked into his algebra class on Friday, and his eyes grew wide with horror as he saw an imposing stack of papers on the teacher's desk.

The midterm! I can't believe I spaced the midterm! His silent screams echoed in his mind.

The tests on Mr. Wilcox's desk stared him down. He thought of explaining what had happened, but Wilcox would never understand. He'd been prepping the class for this test for two weeks. Jeremy was scared. Algebra was his hardest subject. If he could get a B in this course, he'd raise his GPA. But bombing this test would blow any chance of that.

He took his desk and tried a weak smile as Mr. Wilcox placed the paper face down before him. The teacher returned his smile.

"You look relaxed, Jeremy," he said. "Must have this material down, huh?"

"Yeah," Jeremy replied weakly. "No sweat."

He turned to his right to say something to Sam, who also had this class, but Sam wasn't there. Instead Tina Ng, the new Vietnamese student, looked back at him from Sam's seat.

Tina noticed his confusion. "Sam is sick," she explained. "Mr. Wilcox told me to sit here." She was quiet, shy and terribly naive, Jeremy thought. And she also kept her paper in full view of Jeremy. As the bell rang, Mr. Wilcox gave instructions for the test, and the room fell silent except for the scratching of pencil on paper.

Jeremy looked blankly ahead, but to his right he had complete view of Tina's paper. And Jeremy wondered what to do.

What would *you* do?

If Jeremy cheats, turn to page 124.
If he doesn't cheat, turn to page 80.

Barnard Sullivan's one joy in life was his Corvette. It was a 1975 cherry-red, spotless classic which he proudly parked over two spaces of the teachers' lot. Sullivan kept this car perfectly clean as though to say to the school, "You don't have to like me. My car will show you all!" At least that's what Jeremy—amateur psychologist—thought.

When Jeremy walked into class that Thursday, he knew something was wrong. Sullivan was redder than usual and paced like a caged animal in front of the class.

Then, for no reason that Jeremy could tell, Mr. Sullivan exploded in a rage. He started cussing so loud that the guy on the back bench jumped and knocked his tool kit on the floor.

"Pick your tools up, boy!" Sullivan shouted. "I've had it with you wimps! Are you happy? Does it give you pleasure?"

Jeremy turned to a fellow student and raised his eyebrows to ask, "What's up?"

"Don't play innocent with me, Kelly!" Sullivan walked up to him. "You know! Who put shoe polish on my car?" Jeremy flushed red with embarrassment. So that was it—Sullivan's Corvette had been vandalized. Then Jeremy remembered what he'd heard the day before.

Over lunch on Wednesday, Justin Parsons and Matt Brondos had talked about "autographing" the Corvette.

"If he's so squeaky clean, let's help him along with a little polish," Justin said. Jeremy had tried to talk them out of it. Shoe polish can leave permanent marks on a car finish, but the guys didn't listen. Finally, Jeremy gave up and left. But they must've done it.

"You know, don't you? You know who did it!" Sullivan was inches away from Jeremy's face.

Jeremy remained silent. Why should he be responsible for getting those guys into trouble? Still, what they did was wrong. Jeremy pushed his chair back, looked Barnard Sullivan in his red eyes and cleared his throat.

What would *you* do?

If he tells who vandalized the car, turn to page 58.
If he doesn't tell, turn to page 100.

It could be true. Carl Newton could be a homosexual. Jeremy had read how homosexuals worked in all professions, including teaching—and especially the arts. And wasn't English kind of like the arts?

It seemed strange that he had men for roommates, Jeremy thought. Of course, if he had a woman for a roommate, that would be strange too. But he could live alone. Lots of guys live alone. Why didn't Carl Newton?

In the lunchroom Jeremy would watch the way Mr. Newton walked. With a kind of little strut. And then there was that high-pitched laugh.

Hmm, my dad laughs like that too, Jeremy thought. But that's different.

Mr. Newton ate lunch with lots of the male teachers and coached soccer after school. Jeremy later found out it was girls' soccer.

But it was when Mr. Newton came to church on Sunday with his roommate Bob that Jeremy really suspected he was gay. They sat so close. Of course, the church was crowded and everyone was sitting close. Still ...

"I don't know. He's just ... strange, Chris. Maybe you're right."

"Yeah, well, you know. They're all over. My dad says we've got to be real careful."

■

"Homosexuals at Windy Point" read the headline on the school paper the next Friday. The staff had interviewed Jeremy and others, and had published an investigative article that was quite fair. It pointed out that while only one teenager in 1,000 admitted to being homosexual, 3 percent claim to be bisexual and 5 percent reported having had a homosexual experience.

"Certainly there are homosexual students at Windy Point," the article concluded, "possibly even some of the teachers."

Jeremy couldn't believe his eyes! Everyone would know! Sure, he and Chris had mentioned something to the student reporter on Tuesday when she was preparing her article, but he didn't mean ...

On Monday the noise level in the halls was incredible! Everyone was talking, and they were all talking about the same thing. Carl Newton had turned in his resignation over the weekend.

"Although he wasn't attacked directly, he said that the rumors have ruined his teaching career. He's going back to Ohio to be with his fiancee and her family," Trish Hughes said as she grabbed the books from her locker next to Jeremy's.

"His fiancee?!" Jeremy dropped his lunch on the floor.

"Yes, they're supposed to be married next August. I didn't know that. I guess that would've made a difference. In the rumors, you know."

■

"It's my fault, Mom." Jeremy wiped a tear and looked at the floor. The glass of milk in front of him was warm.

"No, not you. Not you alone." Mom was rubbing his arm like she used to when he was little.

"It's called 'homophobia,' Jeremy, and it infects all of us. It's a fear of homosexual people, and it lets rumors like that spread and grow until people get hurt. And it happens all over. Not just at Windy Point."

"I just want to run and hide. Get away from all those jerks."

"It sounds like you want to get away from yourself, Jeremy." Dad had been quiet up to this point.

"Son, we do a lot of talking in church about forgiveness. About how Jesus died to take away our sins. It's not 'sin' just in the general sense, but the specific ones that trouble us." Dad paused and poured another cup of coffee.

"I hope you can let Jesus forgive this sin too, Jeremy. What you did was wrong and someone was hurt. There's a real nasty spirit at Windy Point, and it sounds like it got to you."

"I'm getting out of it. I'm sick of it." Jeremy's voice was low and angry.

"How about doing something about it?" Dad continued. "Maybe you can let this experience give you a new sense of love for people. Remember we talked last week about you running for student council? Maybe this is God's way of telling you to run for office."

"Maybe I just need to get some stuff together, Dad. I've been thinking of asking some kids to get together for a Bible study before school. You can't do much in politics, I guess. Maybe we just need to change some minds first." Jeremy paused. "I don't know. I'm really confused. But I guess I'd like to do something."

What would *you* do?

If Jeremy runs for student council, turn to page 54.
If he starts a Bible study, turn to page 76.

It was one of the most sleepless nights of Jeremy's life. Chris' request to "share" the semester project had been on his mind ever since Jeremy left school.

Cheating was common at Windy Point. "Original" papers were routinely sold in the cafeteria, and the passing of test answers during exams had become a fine art. Jeremy watched during Mr. Richards' last exam as two guys passed papers under the desk while a third kept Mr. Richards distracted.

If it was so common, why did Jeremy feel so uneasy about it? Why not just go along with it?

The next morning before school, Beth Faulkes, the church youth minister, called to remind Jeremy about an upcoming party. It was the only time she knew kids would be home.

"Jeremy, if you sounded any more out of it, you'd be in a coma," she laughed. "Were you asleep?"

"No, I've got something on my mind. That's all."

"So tell me," she said. And the line fell silent as Beth waited.

Slowly, Jeremy explained the situation. He described Chris and how funny (and rich) he was, and how hard it was to find good friends at a new school, and how he knew it wasn't right but everyone did it and he could probably get away with it.

Finally, taking a deep breath, Jeremy said, "Why am I telling you this? You're my youth minister."

Beth laughed. "I also happen to be a human being, Jeremy. And I think I understand how you feel. Look, Jeremy, decisions are rarely easy. We struggle with even the simplest. What do you plan to do?"

"I thought you'd tell me."

"It sounds like you know what's right, but you also know what feels good and what you can get away with."

"It's deciding what's most important that gets me," Jeremy said. "I don't want Chris mad at me. But I don't want Mr. Richards mad at me either. And if my parents found out, they'd be really mad . . . " His voice trailed off.

"How 'bout what you want? What will keep you from being angry at yourself?"

"Huh?" Jeremy was confused. He sat up in his chair.

"You have to live with yourself a lot longer than any of the other people you've mentioned. What should you do to keep peace in your own heart?"

Jeremy grinned. "Thanks, Beth. I'll let you know what I decide."

"I think I already know," Beth said.

■

Chris was at Jeremy's locker, pacing back and forth, when Jeremy got there that morning. He gave Jeremy his warmest, most sincere smile.

"Well, what's the word, Chicago man?"

"The word is 'no,' Chris."

"Huh?" Chris fell back against the next locker. He looked as though someone had hit him in the stomach.

"What do you mean, Jeremy?" Chris asked with pain in his voice.

"You know, Chris, I was a wreck all night trying to figure out what to do. I couldn't get it out of my mind. It made me crazy."

"So why say no?" Chris was still stunned.

"Because," Jeremy placed his hand on Chris' shoulder, "I figured out why I'm so screwed up over this. You see, I'm a Christian, and I look to God to help me make good decisions in my life. It's wrong for me to help you cheat, Chris. I have to do what I think God wants me to do. So the answer is 'no.' " Jeremy was surprised at how relieved he felt.

Chris pushed Jeremy's hand away and took two steps back.

"Well, do you understand?" Jeremy asked, looking at Chris. But Chris just stood there, mouth open. Finally, Jeremy broke the silence.

"We'll talk when we've got more time," Jeremy said. "Right now we've got to get to class. Let's go."

Blind choice:

Without looking ahead, turn to page 111 or page 63 to see what happens to Jeremy's friendship with Chris.

Jeremy did okay on the test. Not great, but okay. His mind kept going back to the slam: geek. That hurt.

Jeremy walked back to his locker, thinking about how he should respond. He opened the locker door and threw his books in the bottom. Then he stood quietly, in thought. Finally, he shook his head.

Ah, it's no big deal, Jeremy thought. When you don't know somebody or want to put them down, you lump them all in the same category. He even called *himself* a "dumb jock."

"Hey, Kelly."

Jeremy turned to see a tall, slender senior coming toward him. He extended his hand and Jeremy shook it, aware of how grubby he must look.

"I'm Scott Cunningham. I'm the newspaper editor."

"Yeah?" Jeremy was confused.

"Mrs. Philby gave me your name. She said you're a good writer."

Jeremy liked the soft-spoken English teacher whose love for books inspired all her students. He felt creative when he wrote for Mrs. Philby.

"Yeah?" Jeremy was still confused.

"We've got an opening on the newspaper staff, and I'd like you to apply. We could use people who like to write. What d'ya say?"

"Well, er, I, uh . . . " Jeremy tried to find a word.

Scott didn't wait for Jeremy to answer. "Look, our next meeting is Wednesday at 3 in the media center. See you there." Then Scott walked away.

"Friendly guy," Jeremy mumbled as he locked his locker. But I guess that's how newspaper people are supposed to act, he thought.

I'm forgetting something, Jeremy kept thinking. What else is going on Wednesday at 3?

"Basketball tryouts!" he said aloud. That was it. He was going to try out for basketball and had a pretty good chance of making at least second string. As a matter of fact, his coach in Chicago had even sent Coach Barnes a letter.

Jeremy knew he couldn't do basketball *and* the newspaper. And even if he tried to, his parents would never allow it.

Jeremy stopped at the stairwell as students breezed passed

him left and right. I've always liked basketball, he thought, but this newspaper thing is something new and different. I don't know which I'd rather do. And I don't have much time to decide.

What would *you* do?

If Jeremy chooses basketball, turn to page 89.
If he joins the newspaper staff, turn to page 92.

The six computer cards felt like feathers in Jeremy's hand. And in fact, that's about what they were worth: English basics, fundamentals of math, health and fitness, current issues, American history and basketball.

■

Jeremy was yawning when he walked into the kitchen and threw his two books on the table.

"Those are all your textbooks?" Mom asked, looking up from her junk drawer. Dad walked in from the living room.

"I decided it's time for a break." Jeremy plopped down at the table. Silence. Only parents can give that kind of silence. They were each looking at him. Waiting.

"I didn't want to pressure myself too much right off." Jeremy tried to sound reasonable. Mom sat down and looked through Jeremy's registration papers.

Dad was standing over him now, looking down. He looked angry. "So, what subjects are you taking, Jeremy?"

Jeremy told them the subjects. Softly, without a lot of emotion. By the time he hit "health and fitness," Dad was glaring.

"What possessed you to deliberately sabotage your school career, Son?" Dad sputtered. "You were laughing at courses like this in Chicago! How do you expect to get into a good college?"

"Who needs it?" Jeremy stood up. "I'm tired of all the pressure! All this 'get ahead and succeed' stuff! Look. Uncle Charlie never went to college, and he's making more money than anyone else in our family!"

That would get him. Dad had always resented his brother's owning a restaurant chain even though he didn't have a college degree.

Mom stepped between them. She was sad. "Jeremy, we don't approve of your course load. And I think the reasons are obvious. You're far more capable than your course load suggests. Now, the instruction paper from school says you have until tomorrow at 3 to change your courses. Either you commit yourself to a more challenging schedule for this fall or . . ." Her voice trailed off as she looked at Dad.

"Or you can forget about any sports!" Dad finished the sentence. That hurt! The basketball coach had talked with him after registration about the team. Dad knew how to go for the pain points!

Jeremy picked up the two books and turned to leave the room.

"I'll think about it," he said softly.

What would *you* do?

If Jeremy takes a heavier course load, turn to page 30.
If he keeps the light load, turn to page 114.

His parents had been hurt by the news, but they were getting over it. He heard them tell some friends at church, "It's his life, and we guess he's got to do what he thinks is best. We're disappointed."

So was he. In a way. At least now he wouldn't have to deal with the pressure. No more tests, book reports, dumb discussions in class.

At first, Jeremy would drop by school in the afternoon—just to see the gang. But later he realized they didn't have that much in common anymore.

He got a part-time job at the convenience store and began saving for a car. He paid his folks $50 a week for room and meals, which left him barely enough to get clothes once in a while. It was okay.

What he really missed was the fun at his locker. Standing around with friends, comparing class notes, talking about the weekend. It was his place, and from there he was going to change the world.

Jeremy stacked a box of candy bars in the store's metal shelving and shook his head. Maybe someday, he thought. Maybe someday I'll go back to school, take some courses that'll really challenge me, and get a better job.

But for now there were customers to serve and television to watch and friends to be with. It was easier.

The End

Jeremy couldn't remember a youth group meeting this intense.

Even Trish, who usually bubbled so loudly you thought she'd explode, sat sullen in the corner, wiping a tear from her eyes. Mr. Newton's resignation had hurt everybody. And Jeremy was hurting more than most.

"I helped spread that rumor about Mr. Newton being gay. I guess I was afraid," Jeremy said. "I was afraid of something I didn't understand."

"We all were, Jeremy," Trish said. "I guess we were all afraid."

"There really is nothing you can do about it, you know," Andrea Lowry said. "It's called 'sin,' and we're all sinners."

Jeremy pulled himself up out of his chair.

"Sure it's sin," he said, "but that doesn't mean we have to give in to it. We can beat it. What would've happened if Jesus had said, 'Yep, that's sin,' and went for a walk? Instead, he died for us. I really think we've got to do something about this!"

"Why don't you run for student council president, Jeremy?" Craig Morris said sarcastically, almost lazily. "Election deadline is tomorrow. You could get yourself elected and then change the whole attitude at Windy Point." Craig smiled his quiet smile and leaned back on a bulletin board.

You could almost feel the atmosphere in the room change. Kids leaned forward, looking at Jeremy. Jeremy felt hot.

"Hey, Craig was joking," Jeremy said. "Student council president is serious business."

"And you're the one to do it, Kelly," Jake Ward said. "You've got recognition and respect, and everyone knows you wouldn't do it for yourself. How about it?"

As a group, the youth group stood and cheered. Jeremy wanted to disappear.

■

Jeremy's opponent in the election was a very large, handsome football player named Chad Swenson. His campaign speeches consisted of talking about himself for five minutes and then saying he'd do his best to improve the food in the cafeteria and get new football uniforms for the team.

COUGARS
M

Jeremy lacked Chad's size and popularity, but Jeremy spoke about attitudes at Windy Point. He talked about changing some of the textbooks that reflected biased attitudes. About how kids needed to respect each other more and care for each other. Some students listened. Others walked away.

■

On election day, Jeremy thought for a moment before dropping his ballot in the box. A gentleman would certainly vote for his opponent, he thought. No, Chad's an air-head. I'd do a better job.

And he cast his vote for himself.

His friends were confident, but Jeremy wasn't sure. All he had going for him was a desire to change Windy Point into a school that cares. Somehow, football uniforms, cafeteria food and a handsome president seemed a better bet.

Blind choice:

Without looking ahead, turn to page 16 or page 40 to see how the election turns out.

It'd been a long, hot summer, but by mid-August Jeremy was glad he'd decided to go to summer school. Things were much more laid-back in summer classrooms than during the regular school year. He'd really appreciated his teachers—they all insisted on being called by first names, and one of them, Alan Richards, even invited the class over to his home for a barbeque the first week of school.

"Summer school is a lot like college," Mr. Richards explained to his class. "You work hard, you learn and you have a good time."

If this was like college, Jeremy was ready!

He'd managed to do a little mechanic work on the weekends, so he had some money in the bank. But the best thing was his GPA. It was a solid 3.2, which meant colleges would begin to take him more seriously.

■

By the middle of his senior year, Jeremy had raised his GPA to a 3.6, and he was narrowing down his choice of colleges. His pastors insisted he look at church schools, but he'd prayed about it and decided he wanted contact with kids from non-Christian backgrounds. The state schools seemed all right, but everybody was going there. And they just didn't seem ... exciting.

Finally, Jeremy heard of a small liberal arts college in Minnesota—Gundermann College. He read their catalog, talked to some kids who went there, and prayed furiously for several weeks to find God's will. Finally, in February, Jeremy was ready to send in his application.

"I won't get accepted," he told his dad as they walked to the mailbox with the thick Manila envelope. "This school takes only the best, and with my GPA, I'm right on the border."

Dad put his hand on Jeremy's shoulder and said, "There are other things, though, Jeremy. You've been really involved in school and active in church. You've got a lot going for you, Son."

Jeremy shrugged and dropped the large envelope in the mailbox. "Here goes nothing!"

Blind choice:

Without looking ahead, turn to page 31 or page 117 to see whether Jeremy is accepted.

Jeremy knew what he had to do, and it was painful. The teacher was surprised to hear that Matt Brondos and Justin Parsons might've been the vandals. Within an hour of Jeremy's tip, Matt and Justin were confronted. They confessed and were put on temporary suspension. Jeremy felt sick.

By Monday morning the word was all over school: Jeremy Kelly had turned in Matt and Justin, and wasn't to be trusted. Jeremy Kelly was out to make points with the faculty. Jeremy Kelly was a welcher.

He tried to explain to the few kids who'd sit with him at lunch.

"It was wrong. Just plain wrong," Jeremy said. "Look, I didn't think they'd really do it."

One girl at the table, Ellen Fields, sneered, "I swear, Jeremy, you used to be so sweet when you came to this school."

"Yeah, maybe you ought to be thinking about your friends once in a while," Gary Carlsen said as he got up. "Matt and Justin don't need three weeks away from school"

"It was wrong," Jeremy snapped.

But Gary and Ellen were walking away, and Jeremy slammed his milk angrily on the table. It splashed onto his hand.

Why bother? he thought. What good does any of this do?

He felt himself getting angry. He'd tried to do what was right, but what did it get him? A table for one the cafeteria.

Maybe they're right—maybe all I should care about is money and getting ahead, Jeremy thought. But . . . there's more than just that. I love learning, and I really do care about people and about doing the right thing.

Jeremy was lost in thought as he walked up to an elderly woman working near the tray conveyor belt.

"Do you go to school for the money you're going to make or because you love to learn?" he asked himself as he set his tray on the belt.

"I beg your pardon?" she gently asked.

Jeremy blushed. "Oh, never mind. It's nothing," he answered.

But in his heart he knew it was everything!

What would *you* do?

If Jeremy stays in school to get a good job, turn to page 105.
If he stays in to learn, turn to page 103.

No big deal.

Even if Mullins wanted to believe Martin Luther was an alien from Planet X, that was Mullins' business. Most kids in the class thought Martin Luther was a civil rights activist in the '60s anyway, and Jeremy was tired of having to do all the fighting for truth.

"The happiest people, in spite of what Beth says," he muttered to himself on the way to class one day, "are those who mind their own business." And that's what Jeremy intended to do.

Minding his own business meant writing word-for-word what Mr. Mullins said, then spitting it back on daily quizzes and tests. It meant holding back when he wanted to contribute in class or question what the teacher was saying.

Eventually, though, Jeremy lost interest in what was once an exciting subject for him. He'd bring comic books to class, concealing them behind his notebook. Because the class was right after lunch, he could sleep easily hidden behind Jason Sweeny, a huge linebacker for Windy Point's football team.

■

"What test?" Jeremy asked.

Trish Hughes looked at Jeremy like he'd lost his mind.

"The semester exam, Jeremy," Trish shouted over the noise in the hallway. "Mullins has been telling us about it for the past week and a half. Where have you been?"

"I've been there, sort of," Jeremy said sheepishly.

"Yeah, we've noticed," Trish responded. "What's been going on with you, anyway?"

"It's boring."

Jeremy was searching his locker for his history book. It was no use. He probably forgot it at home. A test today, huh? It would've helped if he'd read any of the chapters or listened in class, but maybe he could still fake it. If it was multiple choice, he might be able to pass. He'd kind of listened in a couple of classes. Maybe. Maybe.

But it was straight essay.

"Comment on ..."

"What is your understanding of ...?"

"How do you explain ...?"

The questions were meant to demonstrate to Mr. Mullins each student's insight and ability to digest the material he'd presented over the past six weeks—material Jeremy had blocked out of his life. The blank paper in front of him at the end of the hour let him know he'd have some explaining to do at the end of the week.

With the end of the week came the report card: One A, three B's and a C.

And Mullins had awarded him an F for his work in world history. An F! Jeremy had never had an F on a report card before.

As he walked to the front door of his house, he heard the sound of his parents' voices. They were arguing, something they seldom did when he was around. Dad had been under a lot of pressure at work and Mom had been quiet lately.

As he opened the front door, the angry voices stopped suddenly and his parents turned to look at him.

This definitely is no time to get an F on my report card, Jeremy thought.

Blind choice:

Without looking ahead, turn to page 12 or page 72 to see how Jeremy's parents react.

"Ah, the sweet smell of carburetor cleaner!"

Jeremy laughed harder than he'd laughed in months. He was happy. Not only did he not have to spend hours trying to decipher Spanish verb conjugations, he had the joy of doing something totally new and different—which, on this particular Monday afternoon, was figuring out the way a two-barrelled Holley carburetor was put together. He had it spread in front of him, piece by piece, and the smell of the cleaner was getting a little too strong for him. He walked to the window to crack it.

"Hey, you!"

A voice from the front caught him by surprise.

"Just where do you think you're going?"

He turned to look at Mr. Barnard Sullivan, his mechanics teacher. Ex-Marine, ex-race-car driver, and, Jeremy thought, ex-human being.

Sullivan had been the one disappointment in the work-study program. The guys and girls in his Basic Auto Mechanics class were great! He had a paid-intern job at Fisher Automotive, and he was beginning to understand the intricacies of the gas-combustion engine.

But Mr. Sullivan was driving him crazy! The tall buzz-cut teacher fumed into class each morning like a tornado off the plains. He shouted at the students and occasionally called them names.

Jeremy was quick with words, and at first, when he thought Sullivan might be joking with him that day, he tried to joke back.

It was no joke.

Sullivan took him apart. Yelling and screaming. His face red, and the veins in his neck sticking out. Jeremy wondered whether he should walk out of the shop that day. And when Sullivan was through, he sent Jeremy to the principal's office where he sat wondering what he did, until the principal, Mrs. Janet Gill, told him to try to understand Mr. Sullivan.

■

"Understand him?" Jeremy said to the kids at youth group on Sunday night. "This guy's a Neanderthal!"

"Children, respect your parents and others in authority," Jill Martin whined mockingly.

"How about 'Love is patient and kind'?" Beth Faulkes said.

Jeremy pulled himself up from his elbow on the floor.

"Love?" he asked. "It's not so easy with this guy."

"It *is* easy to love the lovable, and hassle-free," Beth said. "It's guys like Mr. Sullivan that challenge us. If Jesus had come to save just the nice guys, he'd have probably spent all his time with them. But he didn't. He was call the 'friend of sinners.' I think God is telling you to start practicing your faith with your teacher, Jeremy."

"You don't know Sullivan, Beth," Jeremy said. "He's a real jerk!"

Beth laughed. "Aren't we all? Some just hide it better than others."

Jeremy really liked Beth. But maybe, here, she was being too . . . holy.

"I've got to do something about Sullivan," he said to the kids. "Maybe Beth is right. Maybe I've got to try to talk to him. But sometimes, a jerk is just a jerk!"

What would *you* do?

If Jeremy confronts Mr. Sullivan, turn to page 107.
If he tries to blow off Mr. Sullivan, turn to page 43.

Jeremy had called Chris three times now, and he was beginning to suspect that Chris would always be angry at him.

Jeremy had explained why he couldn't cheat. He'd even offered to help Chris study for future projects and tests.

But the calls weren't returned. And when Jeremy saw his old friend in the hall, Chris would pretend not to notice. Or he walked the other way.

For weeks Jeremy kept his feelings to himself, but one Sunday morning during Sunday school his feelings came out. The class was talking about friendship.

Sam Anderson was getting excited. "I just don't think you can find the kind of friendship David and Jonathon had. Sorry!"

"That's not true. I've got lots of friends," Robin Feister objected.

"Acquaintances, Robin," Sam corrected. "Lots of acquaintances. A real friend is like Jonathan—someone who'd die for you. Any of your friends ready to die for you?"

"Oh, heavy, man," Craig Morris joked. "Why get so serious?"

"Sam's right," Jeremy said. He'd been quiet for most of the hour. Thinking. "It's hard to find friends—good friends—at Windy Point. People are so interested in what they're wearing, how much money their folks make, and what kind of car they're driving, that what's really important doesn't even get mentioned."

Beth Faulkes, the youth minister, leaned forward. "Sounds like you've found that out personally, Jeremy. Want to talk about it?"

Jeremy took a deep breath. What could he lose? "Yeah, sure. This kid, Chris ..." Some of the others in the group looked at one another. They knew Chris.

"I thought Chris was my friend. He took me around, introduced me to his friends, even said I could use his car." More glances around the room.

"And then he asked me to help him cheat in biology. He wouldn't study. Wouldn't even let me help him."

"So what did you do?" Mark Sims asked.

"I said no. It just wouldn't be right. Now, he ignores me. Won't return my calls. I guess there goes another friendship down the drain."

"So what can we do about that kind of thinking?" Beth asked. "It's not just Chris, as you well know. It's all over your school."

"How about starting a Bible study at school?" Craig suggested. "Maybe kids would come and get their lives straightened out."

Jeremy felt a charge. What a crazy idea! Get the Word out at school, find a classroom early in the morning or after classes, maybe use some of the material they'd used at church. Maybe it could work.

"But who would lead it? They wouldn't let Beth come over."

Beth grinned. "Maybe Beth wouldn't *want* to come over. How about you, Jeremy? Sounds like you've got the greatest frustration. Want to do something about it?"

All heads turned to Jeremy.

"Me? Lead a Bible study at school? Uh, I've got to think this one over!"

What would *you* do?

If Jeremy decides to lead the Bible study, turn to page 110.
If he decides not to lead it, turn to page 65.

"I think it'd be a nice thing for you to do, dear." Jeremy's mom put the stack of bills aside and took off her reading glasses. "You've gained so much out of Bible study. Why not share it with others at school?"

"I don't know, Mom. I'm tired of always being so outspoken about everything." Jeremy wondered if that statement would disappoint his mother.

But Mom smiled. "Jeremy, it's your decision. Just remember that God gives each of us different gifts, and we're responsible to use them wisely."

Jeremy sighed in relief. It was good to know Mom and Dad would support him in any decision. That was one of the reasons he loved them.

Jeremy decided not to lead a Bible study. Instead, he decided to show his Christian faith in less "aggressive" ways. He was tired of always being in the limelight.

■

Jeremy's life was peaceful in the two years that followed. He continued to grow closer to God, but he avoided responsibilities that would draw attention to him at school.

He spent his time getting to know people. He'd been so busy since he'd come to Windy Point that he'd not had many close friends. But now Jeremy was discovering the joys and benefits of getting involved in people's lives—one at a time.

As Jeremy spent time with more and more friends, his popularity grew. It wasn't that he tried to be popular. The other kids just saw something in Jeremy—a fire that made everyone around him feel warm. When asked what made him so different, Jeremy would say it was because he was a Christian. And because of Jesus, God's love flowed through him.

At the end of his senior year, the principal asked Jeremy to lead the prayer at the baccalaureate ceremony—a privilege usually reserved for ministers. This time, Jeremy accepted the offer to be in front of people. He didn't care about being in the spotlight again. He just genuinely wanted to pray for his class.

And, he thought, the prayer would be a fitting thank you to God—for helping him see he didn't always have to do "great things" for God to make a difference in people's lives.

The End

If Chris didn't have the connections, I wouldn't be doing this, Jeremy thought as he grabbed the biology notes from his locker. He'd been up until 1 a.m. putting the finishing touches on the "joint" project by Jeremy Kelly and Chris Miller. Chris had looked at the notes after class the day before and said something like, "Yeah, I guess that's okay. What's an amoeba?"

Jeremy couldn't believe it. If Mr. Richards asked Chris any questions about the project, Jeremy was shot. But there were too many kids, too many projects. He figured he was safe.

He felt bad about deceiving Alan Richards, though. It wasn't like he was cheating, he figured. He was just doing twice as much work and getting half as much credit.

And Chris was paying off. Jeremy was invited to a party at Chris' house on Friday, and he was going. Jeremy had turned down the money, but Chris' Mustang had been promised to him for the homecoming dance as well. And he was hanging out with all of Chris' friends. He felt included. Not a bad reward for sharing credit on one lousy science project.

But Chris had changed. Jeremy had liked Chris at first. Confident and funny. But now Chris seemed darker, more moody and angry a lot. He put down kids for no reason, and Jeremy wondered what Chris was saying about him behind his back.

■

The night before the semester biology exam, Jeremy was pacing the floor of his room memorizing strange-sounding Latin names when the phone rang. His mom called up the stairs, "Jeremy, it's Chris!"

The voice at the other end of the phone sounded like the old Chris—cheerful and cocky.

"Hey, Chicago man, what's happenin'?"

"Hi, Chris! Just studying those lovable biology terms. How about you? Got 'em down?"

"Oh sure, Jeremy. With friends like you, that's no problem."

"Huh?" Jeremy sat on the bed.

"It's like a whole grade depends on tomorrow's test, Jeremy, and I'm calling just to make sure you're willing to help. You've been real good this semester, dude."

Jeremy tried to act dumb, but he knew what Chris wanted. Another exam—and this is the big one.

"Look, Chris, I helped you through the fall project, but that's not like cheating on a major final. I mean, if we're caught on this, we're out!"

"We won't get caught, Jeremy. I got it figured out. I sit behind you. You keep the paper out by the corner of the desk, and I, uh, share with you. It'll work. Trust me."

"No way. Not this time. Chris, you've got to stand on your own sometime. You can't go through life cheating!" Jeremy surprised himself with such a corny sermon.

"Hey, it's your fault, Kelly!" Chris sounded angry and scared. "If you hadn't agreed to help me out with the project, I'd have had to do it on my own. I would've been prepared for this exam. You're responsible for my not knowing this stuff. You owe me this."

Jeremy felt caught. Chris was right in a way. If he hadn't helped Chris cheat, Chris would've had to make it on his own.

"Jeremy, are you studying?" His mother's voice snapped him back to reality.

"Gotta go, Chris. Got to get back to bio." Jeremy wanted to slam the receiver down.

"Well, what about it? Are you going to help me with the test tomorrow or are you going to let me fail? I'm counting on you, Jeremy."

Jeremy sat silently on the edge of the bed. He didn't see any easy answer to this one.

"I'll think about it," he said and hung up.

What would *you* do?

If he lets Chris look at his paper, turn to page 27.
If he refuses to let Chris cheat, turn to page 87.

"I failed."

It was hard for Jeremy to say the words. First, to himself, then to friends. And he didn't want to say them to his parents. But he did.

Jeremy wasn't used to failure. He had been an A-student in Chicago. But maybe he was trying to do too much at once in this new school. Or maybe the stress of moving had affected him more than he thought.

He sat with the algebra test clutched in his hand—an ugly, scummy thing he wished had never happened. He'd had a bad day.

His teacher agreed. "You could do better, Jeremy. But I wonder if you're really putting your best into it."

■

"What's the problem, Son?" Dad asked. He dropped the crumpled test paper on the table as though it were plague-infested.

"How should I know, Dad? I'm 15 years old, and you think I have the answers? I don't know!"

He felt himself getting angry. But he knew that wasn't fair. Dad was trying to help.

"I'm sorry, Dad. It's been a bad day. This school is so competitive. I feel so pressured all the time, and I just don't think I can cut it."

"I know you're trying," Dad said. "I really don't know what I can do to help."

Jeremy sat up. "Well, I've had this one idea floating around in my head lately."

"What's that?" Dad asked.

"I've heard that Windy Point has a great work-study program," Jeremy said softly. "I could take courses in mechanics. You know I've always wanted to learn a trade, even if I did go to college. What do you think about that?"

"I don't know," Dad said. "Are you sure you're not selling yourself short?"

"I don't think so," Jeremy said. "It's not a demotion. Even Jesus was a carpenter, right? And the Apostle Paul made tents. We each have different gifts. I think I'd like the chance to develop some of mine."

"You've really thought about this, haven't you?" Dad said. "I can't make this decision for you, but I trust you to do the right thing."

At that moment, Jeremy genuinely loved his father. He felt free for the first time in a long time, and his dad was giving him permission to make an important choice.

A work-study program in auto mechanics seemed exciting to Jeremy! But then there were his friends at school and church. They might think his going into the program was admitting failure on the more "academic" courses. And he'd be limiting college options if he switched.

He looked down at the F on his algebra test and knew he had an important decision to make.

What would *you* do?

If he stays in the academic program, turn to page 84.
If he switches to the work-study program, turn to page 61.

Jeremy was quiet. His parents' questions confused him. Why *did* he choose those courses?

"You know we only want you to be happy and succeed," Mom said.

Succeed! That word circled around and around in Jeremy's head.

"I didn't do it for you," Jeremy said softly, partly hoping to convince himself. He finished his milk and put down the glass. "Look, I know how important this place is for you and how proud Dad is of this promotion. We're supposed to feel like we're moving up, and I guess I just want to 'move up' too. You know what I mean?"

"Yes, and I'm glad to hear you say that," Dad said. "Too many parents put too much pressure on their kids. Sometimes I wonder how this country's going to make it if we don't stop trying to make our kids grow up too fast!"

Jeremy nodded. He was surprised to see Dad get a little heated. But Jeremy felt proud of his dad for understanding the way things were.

"Your father's right, Jeremy," Mom said. "And if we're giving you the idea you've got to work hard to make us happy, we need to back off."

"Nah, it's not you," Jeremy looked at his plate. "I just want you to be proud of me."

"We're proud of you, Son," Dad said, "but you need time to have fun too. What about extra-curricular activities? Maybe get involved in some of the things you used to do last year."

"How about the basketball team?" Mom suggested. "I read in the school newspaper you brought home that tryouts are next Wednesday. I know you'd enjoy being on the team."

"You've got to be kidding!" Jeremy laughed in disbelief. With all the homework, the papers, the projects, where would he get the time for the team? Chicago was different. He could get his schoolwork done between 7 and 10 each night. But with *this* schedule, it'd be all afternoon and night!

"All right, how about the newspaper or the yearbook?" Dad suggested. "You could get some experience writing. You've always liked to write. Maybe it could help you with some of your other work."

Jeremy shook his head. They just didn't understand. Jeremy

had decided to commit himself to a tough schedule this fall. Maybe it *was* for them. He really didn't know, and it was getting so he didn't care.

Still, his parents' ideas made Jeremy rethink his priorities.

Here he was in a new city with brand new friends. He liked some of the guys on the basketball team. Sure, they weren't Ben and Kenny, but he did need to make new friends. The coach was one of the youth counselors at Jeremy's church. Rumor was he could've had a career in the NBA, but he chose to coach high school instead.

And those kids in English lit. who talked about the newspaper sounded fun! They joked all the time and seemed to have fun working together. Besides, one of the girls was really cute.

Jeremy decided it'd be good to do something to get to know people. But he sure didn't have time for basketball *and* the school newspaper. He had to decide which way to go.

What would *you* do?

If Jeremy goes out for basketball, turn to page 89.
If he gets involved with the newspaper, turn to page 92.

In spite of their bad moods, Jeremy's folks listened to Jeremy's explanation and were sympathetic. So sympathetic, in fact, that Dad had called the principal and asked for an appointment. Jeremy tried to talk them out of it, but they were determined.

■

Mrs. Janet Gill, school principal, had been busy in her office since the Kellys arrived. And the secretary kept making excuses for her. Jeremy's mother was reading a magazine on parenting, and Dad was looking at his watch, tapping his toes. Jeremy felt awkward.

Finally, the door opened and a student left, eyes looking down. Mrs. Gill walked over to them and introduced herself to Jeremy's parents. They entered the small, cluttered office.

"I'm sorry this place is such a mess," Mrs. Gill said. "Please be seated."

Dad was serious, very businesslike, something that was unusual for him. "We don't want to take much of your time, Mrs. Gill," Dad said, "but we've heard why Jeremy flunked his world history class, and we think it's unfair. We want the grade changed." One thing about Dad, Jeremy thought—he gets right to the point.

Over the next half-hour, Jeremy and his parents explained to the principal why he'd failed the course. They told of the argument about Martin Luther, of the discouragement that followed. Jeremy explained why he'd withdrawn into himself and lost interest. Finally, Mrs. Gill breathed a long sigh and spoke.

"I've talked with Mr. Mullins about you, Jeremy, and his story is different. He sees you as lazy and uninterested in world history, something I have a hard time believing in light of your past grades and your explanation."

Jeremy smiled.

"However . . . I can't change the grade."

Jeremy stopped smiling. His father sat forward, ready for an argument.

She continued. "Once a teacher makes a decision, we have to back the teacher. It's our policy at Windy Point, and I have to enforce that policy. You should've come to see me when the problem started."

Jeremy's mother had been silent throughout the conversation. Now she cleared her throat and spoke.

"Mrs. Gill, as Christians we're committed to our son being able to express his faith in his everyday life. We're also committed to everyone—no matter what they believe—being able to express their individual beliefs, no matter what they are, in their own way. We feel that Jeremy's expression of his faith was mocked by Mr. Mullins, and we'd like you to assure us that it will not happen again—not to Jeremy nor to any other student at Windy Point."

Mrs. Gill was silent. She looked embarrassed and awkward, something that Jeremy had never seen in her before.

"I will speak with Mr. Mullins, and with all of our faculty members about that, Mrs. Kelly. Jeremy's grade will have to stand, but I can assure you that from now on the religious faith of our students will be respected in Windy Point's classes."

As they left the campus, Jeremy felt great love for his parents. He had long-respected their faith. Now he saw it in practice, and it made him proud.

"Thanks, Mom . . . Dad. You were great in there," he said.

"The next time, stand up and fight, Son," Dad said, giving him a playful shove. "Turkeys come in all sizes and ages. Even adults can use a good dose of the truth."

"I'll remember that the next time we get in an argument, Dad."

And his dad chased him all the way to the car.

The End

As he approached Mr. Wilcox's desk, Jeremy knew he was in trouble. The old man took off his glasses, rubbed his bushy eyebrows and looked up at him, speaking quietly. "Young man, I've been in this business a long time." Jeremy shifted back and forth from one foot to the other, unable to look the teacher in the eyes. Behind him he felt 48 eyes burning into his back.

Mr. Wilcox whispered so that only Jeremy could hear. "I think I can spot a student cheating with one eye closed, and I've seen you over the last half-hour copy Miss Ng's paper from top to bottom. I was hoping I was wrong, but I doubt it. Why not go back to your seat as though nothing has happened and finish your test on your own? I'll see you at 2:45 in my office, and we'll go from there."

Jeremy was grateful to Mr. Wilcox for sparing him the shame, but he dreaded 2:45.

At 2:45, Jeremy approached Mr. Wilcox's office with the same fear as he had at the teacher's desk earlier. The door was open, and Wilcox was quiet as he motioned Jeremy to a chair against the wall. The teacher was quiet for the longest time. Jeremy kept looking down, growing more warm by the minute.

"Well, why did you do it?" Mr. Wilcox broke the silence.

"Do what?" Jeremy asked.

"Don't play games with me, Son!" Mr. Wilcox spoke so loudly Jeremy jumped and dropped his books. He picked them up slowly.

"Yeah, you're right. I cheated," he said. "I didn't have time to study and I need a 3.5 to make sure I get into college."

"And this is the way to do it?" Mr. Wilcox leaned back in his chair as he spoke.

"I'm not the only one, you know," Jeremy said. "Lots of kids cheat. I can name other kids in that class who do the same thing I did, but they don't get caught."

"I wouldn't be so sure about that," Mr. Wilcox said. "You're not the first to be here, and I doubt you'll be the last. But numbers don't make right and wrong. What concerns me is you, Jeremy."

Jeremy sensed the gentleness in the big man's voice. Maybe he'd get off easily. "What?" Jeremy asked. "Do you mean you'll let me go? I promise—I'll never do it again."

"Perhaps," the teacher said, "but if you go through life short-cutting and cheating, you won't learn to appreciate much in life." Mr. Wilcox paused. "I'm not going to report you, Jeremy."

Jeremy breathed a sigh of relief.

"You are." Mr. Wilcox picked up the phone on his desk, punched a square button and handed it to Jeremy.

"Call one of your parents and tell them what you've done. I'd like a conference with you and them tomorrow afternoon." Mr. Wilcox stood and left the room.

Jeremy dialed his number slowly and deliberately. As he dialed, he prayed silently, Lord, I know you tried to stop me from doing this. I'm sorry. I only pray that next time . . . I'll listen.

The End

"Uh, don't get me wrong, Jeremy."

Mr. Johnson ran his hand over what had once been a head of hair.

"I'm very much in favor of the Bible. But the matter of church-and-state separation enters in here, and we could have a lawsuit on our hands if you insist on having that Bible study on school property."

"Yeah, I know. But I really think a Bible study would benefit the school. I think it could really turn some people around and get them on the right track. And I think equal access should allow for a Bible study."

Mr. Johnson didn't look convinced.

"Okay, Mr. Johnson. How 'bout this. You allow us to have the Bible study for one semester. I'll give you regular reports of who's coming and what we talk about. If, at the end of the semester, you don't think it's a worthwhile group, we'll quit."

Mr. Johnson sat motionless for a minute. Then, without the slightest expression, he said, "Okay. One semester. We'll work out the details."

■

Word spread quickly that a Bible study open to all students at Windy Point was to have its first meeting next Wednesday at 7 a.m. in Room 224. By Monday afternoon, kids were coming up to Jeremy in the hall to ask questions:

"What's the point?"

"You some kind of religious nut?"

"Who's going to lead it?"

Jeremy kept answering, "Come and see," but he wasn't sure what the answers were. He just knew that someone had to do something, and he was the guy. It was crazy.

■

Jeremy was up at 5:45 on Wednesday, dressed and out the front door by 6:30—with a Bible under one arm and his backpack over his shoulder. The school was brightly lit, and Craig and Trish were already in the room arranging chairs in a circle.

By 6:50 kids started to filter in, still sleepy, but rowdy and pushing. At 7:00 the place was full, and by 7:05 several kids were even seated on the floor.

"Hey, Jeremy," Craig shouted above the noise. "Either you organize something, or we start doing aerobics."

"I think this is going to work!" Jeremy said aloud to himself. "I really think this crazy thing is going to work!"

Blind choice:

Without looking ahead, turn to page 34 or page 36 to see how the Bible study turns out.

Jeremy always loved Saturday mornings—whether in Chicago or in Denver. This Saturday he slept until 10, then drifted downstairs to the sound of his dad mowing the lawn—something that was supposed to be his job.

"Your father felt sorry for you, I guess," Mom said as she cracked two eggs into a hot frying pan. "I think he secretly likes the exercise, though."

The morning paper was open on the table in front of him, and as he turned toward the sports page and the ball scores, his eye caught a photograph of the Windy Point field house with a bulldozer crashed through the wall.

"Oh no!" Jeremy gasped.

Mom turned. "What's wrong, dear?"

"Uh, nothin', Mom," he said. He read the brief article under the headline: "Vandals Destroy Field House."

"A large construction bulldozer found its way into the Windy Point field house late Friday night or early Saturday morning, destroying much of the south side of the building."

"They did it," Jeremy muttered to himself. "Those crazy guys did it!" Jeremy figured either they were more destructive than he thought, or the machine went out of control. He wondered if Justin and Matt were all right.

The back door slammed shut as Jeremy's father walked into the kitchen. He wiped his forehead and looked at Jeremy over his sunglasses.

"So, Prince Charming riseth to greet the dawn."

Jeremy barely looked up from the newspaper.

"What's so interesting, Son?" Dad asked. Then he saw the article. He'd read it earlier.

"I think someone's in big trouble," Dad said. "That's major damage."

Jeremy knew that Matt and Justin had planned a harmless prank—one he almost joined in on. He sat silently, playing with the eggs on the plate in front of him.

Dad looked at Jeremy suspiciously. "Jeremy, do you know anything about this?"

"No, not really. I don't know anything." Jeremy hated lying to his parents, but this was serious. Then the telephone rang, and Jeremy sighed in relief.

Dad talked on the phone in the hallway for a few minutes,

then returned to the kitchen. "It's Mr. Barnes for you, Jeremy. He said he thought he saw you and two other guys by the field house yesterday, looking at that bulldozer. He wonders if you might know anything about last night's vandalism. I think you'd better talk to him, Son."

Jeremy started to say something about not wanting to, but that would seem suspicious. He pushed aside his plate and walked toward the telephone. He wondered what he'd say.

What would *you* do?

If he tells the coach who did it, turn to page 58.
If he doesn't tell, turn to page 100.

"Jeremy, time for dinner!"

Jeremy was lost in the oblivion of Beatles tunes as he lay on his bed, his Walkman cranked up high. He'd had a hard day and needed to unwind.

Mom cracked open Jeremy's bedroom door and smiled. "Kitchen to music man," she called out. "Come in, music man."

Jeremy looked up and pulled his headphones off.

"Time for dinner, dear," Mom said.

Dad had come in earlier, but Jeremy wasn't ready to talk about his test then. As a matter of fact, he wasn't ready now, but he knew he'd have to face up to it. He loved just listening to his music. He figured it was the one way he could still relax.

"You've been in your room since you got home from school," Dad said between bites of spaghetti. "Did you have a rough day?"

"Yeah." Jeremy played with his pasta. "It's the algebra test. I barely passed," Jeremy said listlessly. "It's not that I don't understand it. I'm just under too much stress. I can't seem to keep all my bases covered."

"So what are you going to do about it?" Mom gently responded. She was good at throwing the problem back to him.

Jeremy sighed.

"Well, Mr. Campbell asked me today if I wanted to switch to a work-study program. We were talking about my classes and how much stress I'm under. I told him I'd much rather be out making money, and he said he could likely arrange something at Fisher Automotive over on Jasmine Street. They hire work-study kids all the time, and it'd be a great way to learn a trade."

"And judging what Bob charged me for my last tune-up, you could be a wealthy man in no time," Dad laughed.

Mom put down her glass. "So what do you want to do, Jeremy?"

"I don't know. It's like everybody sees the work-study kids as real idiots, but I know some of them. They're smart but not in the way other kids are."

"You'd be closing the door on college, you know," Dad said.

"And you wouldn't have time for many of your school responsibilities anymore," Mom added.

"I'm not having much effect on school policy," Jeremy sighed. "And why spend your money for college if I'm going to drop out anyway? I'm just not sure college is for me. And I'd really like to learn a trade like mechanics. But I don't know if that's what I want to do with the rest of my life."

"Well, you know we'll support you whatever you decide," Mom said. "Just be sure you're doing what you think is right for yourself and for God."

"Okay, Mom," Jeremy said. "I will."

What would *you* do?

If Jeremy stays in the academic program, turn to page 84.
If he switches to work-study, turn to page 61.

Jeremy didn't feel very close to Pastor Hughes, the senior pastor at his church. He always seemed busy. Besides, the youth minister, Beth Faulkes, was always there for the kids, so Jeremy spent most of his church time with her and other kids.

Jeremy was really surprised when Beth told him to talk to Pastor Hughes. "Most teachers are there to help you, Jeremy. This guy sounds like a sour apple, but I think you should talk with Pastor Hughes to get his opinion before you do anything," Beth said.

■

Jeremy thought Pastor Hughes would have a more impressive office. It was small and cluttered. When he apologized for the way it looked, Jeremy said, "Ah, that's okay. It kinda looks like my room." He wondered if that was a good thing to say.

Jeremy told the pastor about the confrontation with Mr. Mullins.

"He wouldn't accept the truth, Dr. Hughes," Jeremy said. "Of course the Protestant Reformation was about religion. Why'd he get so angry?"

"Well, it's your version of the truth, Jeremy. And we have to remember: A public school system must allow for a lot of different perspectives."

Jeremy nodded.

Pastor Hughes continued. "Still, this gentleman seems to go a bit overboard. Some people can be pretty closed-minded when it comes to religion. I'd think a good teacher would want to encourage healthy debate."

"Not him," Jeremy said. "He just wanted me to sit quietly and listen. And none of the other kids tried to help me either."

Pastor Hughes leaned back in his chair and sighed. "So what do you want to do, Jeremy?"

"I was hoping you'd tell me."

"Can you talk to the principal? Will she listen?"

"To me? A lowly student? You'd have to be student council president or something."

"So run for student council president," Pastor Hughes smiled. But the wheels in Jeremy's head suddenly went into overdrive.

■

Jeremy didn't have much time to put a campaign together. He convinced a couple of people on the school paper—Sam Anderson and Tyra Segars—to help with some signs and passing out leaflets. They even came up with the slogan: Jeremy—He'll Make a Difference.

"It doesn't rhyme, but it says something," commented Tyra, smiling at Jeremy as usual. Jeremy's two opposing candidates were Chad Swenson—good-looking, and a player on the football team—and Tiffany Griffin—a cheerleader and honor student.

"Their idea of a platform is something you dance on," Sam commented. "You're the only one who has anything to say."

And he was right. As nice as Chad and Tiffany were, they really didn't stand for much. Jeremy promised to work for greater openness in the classroom, for student representation on faculty committees, and for a faculty-student task force to evaluate several of the textbooks the school used.

Tiffany thought a senior "ditch day" could be fun, and Chad wanted to redecorate the locker rooms.

Elections would be on Friday morning, and by Thursday afternoon Jeremy was nervous. He stood at the south door wearing a big button that said "Jeremy," shaking hands as kids left.

By 4 the halls were empty and Jeremy, Tyra and Sam were pulling down their posters and peeling masking tape off the walls.

"Well, we tried," Jeremy said.

"Hey, the election hasn't even begun," Tyra said. "You're talking like you've lost."

Sam ripped a sign in two. "I think they'd much rather have their locker rooms decorated. We may be too serious for them."

The three friends walked out of the building toward the bus stop in silence. "Hey, thanks a lot," Jeremy said to them as the bus pulled up. "I really appreciate your help."

"Better start writing your acceptance speech, Jeremy," Sam laughed.

Tyra just smiled at Jeremy as she boarded the bus.

Blind choice:

Without looking ahead, turn to page 16 or page 40 to see how the election turns out.

Monday morning found Jeremy back in the same old classes with a new attitude. He knew the pressure would return, but with consistent study and a positive outlook—not to mention the help of his parents and friends—he felt he could handle it. Quizzes, tests and papers came in a fury, but he tackled them one at a time. And by the end of the semester, he was pulling an A average. His folks were proud, teachers were encouraging and Jeremy felt good about himself.

In the middle of Jeremy's junior year, Mr. Campbell, Jeremy's grade-level adviser, began to encourage him toward college. "You're a good student, Jeremy. The grades speak for themselves. And the SAT exam is just a few weeks away. I know you can do well on it."

"I think I can too, Mr. Campbell," Jeremy said. "The question is whether I want to go to college. I know everybody says you're supposed to, but it may not be for me. I've been thinking about just learning a trade, maybe auto mechanics."

"Well, you know the statistics. On the average, a high school graduate will earn a little over $1,000 a month while a college grad earns close to $2,000 a month. From a dollars-and-cents point of view, college makes a lot of sense."

"But what if I find it's not for me? I don't want my folks spending lots of money on me if I'm going to drop out."

"That's something to consider. College is expensive, and a lot of kids get disillusioned by what they find when they go. If that's what's going to happen, you'd be better off going to a trade school or taking a job."

Mr. Campbell got up from behind his desk and handed Jeremy a pale-blue registration booklet.

"Here are the registration forms for the SAT exam. Why not talk it over with your parents and drop the application off at my office on Monday? Or if you decide you don't want to go to college, just toss it."

Jeremy took the booklet and stared at it. He'd put off this decision for a long time. He wished someone could make it for him.

What would *you* do?

If Jeremy decides to go to college, turn to page 21.
If he decides not to go to college, turn to page 123.

Chris' accusation of Mr. Newton continued to bother Jeremy. But he figured he couldn't do much about the situation, whether or not Mr. Newton was gay. So why worry? Nice and logical. He wouldn't even think of it.

That is, until Sunday morning when Mr. Newton and his friend, a tall muscular guy showed up at church.

Jeremy spent most of the service looking at the two men two rows in front of him. They obviously knew the hymns and service order. They stood when they were supposed to and bowed their heads on cue. And when the service was over, the English teacher looked at Jeremy and smiled. Jeremy felt uneasy.

Beth smiled too when Jeremy told her of his concern.

"So Chris says Mr. Newton's gay." Beth said both as a question and statement. "And how does he know?"

"Chris just knows. He gets around."

"Maybe he is gay. Maybe he isn't. What difference does that make in the way you treat him?"

"It's just, you know, weird. I've never met a gay guy before."

"And you may not be meeting one now, Jeremy." Beth's voice was intense. "Look. Jesus hated sin, just as God does. But he loved people. Jesus loved all kinds of people when he walked this Earth. Even those—especially those—others rejected. I wonder how Jesus would treat Mr. Newton."

Jeremy hated it when Beth confronted him. But he knew she was right.

After a pause, Beth continued, "Homosexuality is a serious charge to throw at anyone, Jeremy. Have you talked to Mr. Newton about the rumors you're hearing?"

"Talk to him?" Jeremy hadn't thought of that. But it began to seem to be the best thing to do.

■

Jeremy found Carl Newton sitting in his office, feet on his desk, reading a book. He put the book down as Jeremy knocked and entered the cluttered, small office.

Mr. Newton smiled gently and extended his hand. "You're Jeremy Kelly. I saw you in church on Sunday, but you looked like you were pretty busy. Sorry I didn't talk to you."

"Er, yeah, Sunday school started early," Jeremy lied. He was just feeling too awkward to talk with Mr. Newton on Sunday.

"My roommate and I have been meaning to get to your church before, but we've been so busy on Sunday. Here, sit down." He pointed to a chair. Jeremy nervously sat down.

"Back in Ohio I was really active in church. My fiancee and I were both youth directors."

Jeremy sat up straight. "Your fiancee? That's like a girlfriend?"

Mr. Newton laughed. "That's like a super girlfriend! Here's a picture." He pointed to a gold-framed picture of a pretty young woman.

"She's coming out in July, and we plan to be married next August. Hey, are you all right? You look sick."

Jeremy was beet-red, feeling so many emotions. Relief, amusement and shame. He was really embarrassed.

"Yeah, I'm okay. I was just wondering if you'd like to recommend some books for my English paper. I'd like to surprise Mrs. Philby, and I figure you might have some ideas."

Mr. Newton talked with Jeremy that afternoon, and on Sunday he brought some books to church.

Jeremy liked the eccentric young teacher. He was bright and curious, and a very dedicated Christian who thought of being a writer someday.

■

"Say, Kelly, you and Newton are spending a lot of time together lately, aren't you?" Chad Swenson, a popular football player, stopped at Jeremy's locker on his way out of school that next Thursday.

"Yeah. He's helping me with my English paper. So?"

"So I guess you're one of them too." Chad was smiling.

"When his fiancee arrives in July, you'll stop saying those things."

Chad gave a look that said, "Yeah, right" and walked away.

Before long, Jeremy began to notice kids talking about him. Snickers in the hallway. Even some of his friends seemed to be avoiding him. Or was it his imagination? He liked Carl Newton, but he also liked his own reputation.

What would *you* do?

If Jeremy ignores the rumors and ridicule, turn to page 10.
If he withdraws from the kids, turn to page 96.

It was one of the longest nights of Jeremy's life. Jeremy couldn't help thinking about Chris' insane request.

To "share" my answers! Can you believe that idiot? Jeremy thought to himself as he threw himself on the living room couch.

"Are you all right, Son?" Dad asked from behind the sports section.

"Uh, sure, why do you ask?"

"You just seem preoccupied. That's all."

Dad—Jeremy had long suspected—possessed mind-reading skills.

Jeremy shook his head. "No, it's nothing. Some stuff I've got to work out by myself."

Mom and Dad would be shocked to learn of the cheating that went on at Windy Point. "Original" papers were routinely sold in the lunchroom, and passing test answers during exams had become a fine art. Jeremy watched during Alan Richards' last exam as two guys passed papers under the desk while a third kept the teacher distracted.

So if it was so common, why did Jeremy feel so uneasy? Why couldn't he just go along?

Then it hit him! He slammed his hands down into the cushion and sat up straight. Dad looked over the papers again. Jeremy pulled himself to his feet and went up to his room to study for the biology exam.

■

Chris was at the locker, pacing back and forth, when Jeremy got there the next morning. He gave Jeremy his warmest, most sincere smile.

"Well, what's the word, Chicago man?"

"The word is 'no,' Chris."

"Huh?" Chris fell back against the next locker. He looked as though someone had hit him in the stomach.

"What do you mean, Jeremy?" Chris asked with pain in his voice.

"You know, Chris, I was a wreck all night trying to figure out your stupid request. I couldn't get it out of my mind. It made me crazy."

"So why say no?" Chris was still stunned.

"Because," Jeremy placed his hand on Chris' shoulder, "I figured out why I'm so screwed up over this. You see, I'm a Christian, and I look to God to help me make good decisions in my life. It's wrong for me to help you cheat, Chris. I have to do what I think God wants me to do. So the answer is 'no.' " Jeremy was surprised at how relieved he felt.

Chris pushed Jeremy's hand away and took two steps back.

"Well, do you understand?" Jeremy asked, looking at Chris. But Chris stood there, mouth open.

Finally, Jeremy broke the silence. "We've got a test to take, Chris. Let's get going."

Blind choice:

Without looking ahead, turn to page 63 or page 111 to see what happens next.

Coach Barnes was hard on his players, but that was nothing new to Jeremy. In his old school, drills and practices were three hours long each day, and Jeremy loved the rigor. It kept him in great shape, and he liked the guys on his team. He was just ready to qualify for second string when the family left Chicago, and Coach Myer had let him know he could be first string if he tried hard enough.

But the team at Windy Point was in a larger conference and played against more competitive schools. Still, Jeremy made the second string with no trouble.

"Bob Myer was right about you," Coach Barnes told Jeremy after practice one day. You've got great potential, Jeremy, and I can see you on my first string within a year." Jeremy couldn't believe it!

Jeremy was only 5 feet 11 inches, but he was fast and had a great shooting arm. Opposing guards would ignore him until he dropped his third basket. Then they'd see him as a threat. Jeremy loved it!

But basketball took a lot of time. Coach Barnes insisted that basketball was life at Windy Point. For the first month Jeremy was exhausted when he dragged in at 6 for dinner and family devotions. He'd try to stay awake to study, but more than once he fell asleep in the middle of algebra problems.

Two weekends in a row of "away" games finally forced Jeremy to go to the coach. One was an overnight. The other was a Saturday-night game, and the team didn't get home until midnight. With church the next morning and an afternoon of study, Jeremy could hardly get out of bed for school on Monday.

"Coach, when will this schedule let up?" Jeremy asked after practice that afternoon. "I'm getting worried about my grades."

The coach frowned. "If you're worried, I'm worried, Jeremy. If we keep winning, our schedule will only get heavier as we move to the tournament. You're good, Jeremy, but you still need more work to make first string. I need you to hang in there."

Jeremy looked down at the gym floor. "I flunked my first test ever last week, Coach. My first one. I fell asleep after school and didn't study. That puts my algebra grade in the D range. I've got to get that grade up."

"I wish I could help you, Jeremy," Coach Barnes said. "But you've got to make some decisons. I hope you stick with basket-

COUGARS
1
BEARS
3
BEARS
4

ball. The team really needs you. But if you flunk, you won't be able to play anyway. You know the rules."

Coach Barnes walked out of the gym toward his office. Jeremy picked up the basketball at his feet, bounced it a couple of times and threw it in a high spinning arch toward the basket a half-court away. It swished neatly through the hoop.

He looked around. An empty gymnasium. Nobody had seen it.

"If only school was that easy," Jeremy laughed to himself.

What would you do?

If Jeremy quits the team, turn to page 121.
If he keeps trying to make it work, turn to page 14.

The journalism offices were in a brightly lit wing of the media center, a separate building on the high school campus. The others on the staff were clever and fun. When they discovered that Jeremy could take their kidding and stand up for himself, they accepted him.

The "Journies," as they called themselves, were an independent bunch. They all pretty much did their own thing. The editor, Scott Cunningham, sat like a statue in front of the computer terminal, grinding out articles for the paper. And then there was Tyra Segars, a beautiful, funny girl who always smiled when Jeremy looked at her. This has possibilities, Jeremy thought.

Still, Jeremy knew it would take time to fit in. He did what Scott told him to do, tracking down stories of the Spanish Club car wash, the choir's proposed tour to Mexico and the schoolwide "Olympics of the Mind" project.

Jeremy started to really enjoy the writing. His adrenalin flowed every time a deadline approached. And he enjoyed getting absorbed in the story on the computer screen in a dark corner of the office.

When he walked into the office one Friday afternoon, Scott motioned him over and told him to sit down.

"Jeremy, we just got this," Scott said and handed him a memo from the principal's office.

"Beginning October 1, Windy Point High School will begin utilizing drug dogs in an effort to stem illegal drug use on the school grounds," the memo began. It went on to explain the concern of the Parents Council regarding drug use at the school and mentioned a recent bathroom "raid" in which 12 seniors were busted for using marijuana.

"What do you think?" Scott asked.

"It's unfair!" Jeremy said. "Those 12 guys have been in and out of trouble all year long. Why should the rest of us have to be humiliated because of them? No way! The crazy Parents Council leaders see drug pushers everywhere they look!"

"How 'bout an editorial for the next issue?" Scott asked. "We'll cut the piece on the choir tour and expand the editorial page to give you a 'guest spot.' Okay?"

Jeremy was flattered but tried not to show it. On the way home, he grabbed some statistics at the library about teenage drug use. Then he spent the weekend in his room writing the editorial. On Sunday night he had a long talk with his parents, who supported the drug-search program. They debated with him; but in the end, they gave him a hug and congratulated him on a good piece that stated his point of view strongly.

The papers arrived at the media center on Thursday afternoon, and Jeremy was first in line to pop the band that held the pile. He flipped to the editorial page, and his mouth dropped open. The choir-tour piece took the top half of the page, and Scott's weak little editorial about no chocolate milk in the lunchroom finished out the page. Not one word about the drug dogs! It had been cut! And Scott hadn't said a word.

At that moment, Mr. Johnson—the school's assistant principal and the paper's supervising editor—walked in with Scott. Scott looked embarrassed.

"I know what you're thinking, Jeremy," Scott said. "It was out of my hands."

Jeremy scowled. Why didn't he tell me? Jeremy thought.

Mr. Johnson walked over to Jeremy. "Sorry, Jeremy. It was a well-written editorial, but I couldn't let it run. There are some things we don't discuss in this paper, and a decision of the Parents Council is one of them. I couldn't let you question it. It'd cause too much trouble in the student body."

"That's not fair!" Jeremy exploded. "First you encourage us to express our opinions; then when we do, you censor us. That's unfair, Mr. Johnson. That's really wrong."

"We don't censor all you write," Mr. Johnson replied. "But there are limits to what student newspapers can do. And we had to draw the line here." Scott stood looking down at the floor.

"I don't know if I can stay on a staff where that's the policy," Jeremy said, getting control of himself.

Scott spoke quietly. "Jeremy, don't quit over this. I don't agree with Mr. Johnson either, but walking away won't change anything."

Jeremy looked at the computer terminal covered by his notes. It was wrong, and his quitting would make a point. But he did like this place. A lot.

What would *you* do?

If Jeremy quits, turn to page 19.
If he stays, turn to page 17.

Somewhere inside, Jeremy knew he needed to hang on. He heard something telling him he could do it.

When school started again that Monday, Jeremy focused on getting back to the routine of being a student. Mom said it was like going to work. Sometimes she didn't want to, but she did anyway. Regular hours, no interruptions.

The basketball season was over, so there was no distraction there. And the kids at church knew that Jeremy needed to work hard, so they left him alone. He got up early enough to be in class on time and learned to use study hall well. The papers that used to be stuffed into his backpack were now neatly filed in stiff Manila folders in his desk. And he kept an assignment book in the outer pocket of his backpack. "Write it down!" was Beth's advice. She was one of the most organized people he knew.

Jeremy wondered why he'd let his studies get so far away from him that he'd actually considered dropping out. By treating study like a job, he was able to get the assignments done each day and still have time to be with his friends and family.

It was starting to show in his grades too. His history grade had come up to a C and was still moving up. Algebra and biology test scores were rising, and Jeremy felt good not only about his grades but about himself. He was more fun to be around. His parents could joke with him again—something that hadn't been possible recently.

The Bible study the following Sunday morning was about motivation: Why do you do what you do?

"So why the big change in Jeremy Kelly?" Trish Hughes asked. "Let's take a deep look into your soul."

Jeremy laughed. "I don't know. I just had to change. It was either work or flunk, and I guess I chose to get busy. It's paying off too."

Josh Peterson pushed. "But why do you bother? How come you're so big on getting good grades? I figure kids study either for money or to learn something. Why do you study?"

"I don't know," Jeremy said, pulling himself up off the floor. "I never thought about it. What difference does it make?"

"Well, for one thing," Josh said, "if you're in it to be a success, you'll play the game. Play up to teachers, and forget about doing what you want to do."

"But if you really want to learn something," Trish continued, "you'll explore more on your own. Read good books just because they're good, not because someone requires them. Actually learn something."

Jeremy had always admired Trish for her free spirit. And she was a good student too.

"I really don't know why I'm studying," Jeremy said. "I guess I should think about it."

So he did. For the next few weeks Jeremy evaluated his motives for learning. He wanted to know what he was in this for—money or education.

What would *you* do?

If Jeremy decides he's studying to make money, turn to page 105.
If he decides he's studying to learn, turn to page 103.

The mustard from his bologna sandwich dripped onto his algebra book, and Jeremy wiped it quickly, carefully, never looking up from the page.

The noise in the lunchroom was almost deafening, but Jeremy was in his own world, a world he'd entered two weeks ago in anger and disgust.

"If they're going to act this way," he said to himself, "I'll just stay to myself."

And he did. From morning until night, Jeremy kept to himself, keeping his attention on his books and his family. Old friends thought he was sick at first. Later they were confused and finally figured that Jeremy was stuck-up—that he felt he was too good for others.

At first, Jeremy didn't mind his self-imposed loneliness. But after the second week, the novelty of being alone in the midst of others wore off and he began to feel all alone. He remembered that feeling from his first weeks in his new home, and he didn't like it.

But he'd taken a stand, and he wouldn't back down. He would survive alone in the midst of uncaring, unfeeling people. That would show them!

He looked up with his mouth full of sandwich to find a crowd of kids staring down at him—Trish Hughes, Andrea Lowry, Mark Sims, Jake Ward, Craig Morris, Sam Anderson and a few others. All standing very quietly, looking down at him. He felt like a jerk with his mouth full of bread and bologna, a bit of mustard dripping down his chin.

"So what's the problem, guy?" Craig asked. "You won't talk to us! You won't look at us! If you want to be a monk, find a cave. But, we'd like an explanation. And if we don't get one ..."

The kids each pulled out from behind their back a can of shaving cream.

"You'll be sorry!" Craig continued, aiming the nozzle at Jeremy.

Jeremy laughed so hard he thought he'd choke on the sandwich!

So Jeremy explained to his friends what he'd been feeling, why he'd secluded himself. And they understood. So Jeremy decided to re-enter life at Windy Point.

■

"Look, I'm in trouble," Chris told Jeremy. Chris was Jeremy's biology lab partner. He was rich and used to getting his way.

"It's like I've wasted this whole quarter, and the biology test is day after tomorrow."

"You want me to help you study?" Jeremy asked. "I've got that stuff down cold! I'll come over tonight."

"No, I've got a date. I can't get the time free." Chris looked worried. "All you got to do is keep your paper on the right side of your desk. We'll sit behind Mike Andrews. He's big, and Richards can't see over him. Just keep your eye on Richards, and let me share your answers. Okay?"

Jeremy looked confused. "I don't know. It isn't right."

"Look, you can even borrow my car for the homecoming dance. C'mon, man, I need help!" Chris looked desperate.

■

The classroom was quiet and Alan Richards looked tired. He had a stack of journals he paged through during the test. Jeremy was sure he and Chris were okay. Jeremy would write the answer, move behind Mike Andrews' huge back and slide the paper to the upper right of his desk. He could feel Chris move silently over his right shoulder.

Finally the bell rang, and a loud sigh rose from each person in the room. Papers were passed forward and there was a mass groan as kids walked out of the room. Chris and Jeremy walked to the front of the room and toward the open door.

"Jeremy. Jeremy Kelly." Mr. Richards' voice cut though the confusion. Jeremy and Chris turned to look at him.

"Guys, I'd like to have a word with you," Alan Richards said.

Blind choice:

Without looking ahead, turn to page 23 or page 125 to see what happens to Jeremy.

"Daddy!"

Amanda ran through the room on her 3-year-old legs and wrapped her arms around Jeremy's legs.

How in the world she could get such speed in such a small apartment always amazed him. He dropped his books on the floor and the two of them picked them up together. Then he scooped his daughter in his arms and walked into the kitchen to kiss Susan.

Jeremy had married Susan just out of college. It was rough being in graduate school with a small family, but Jeremy loved every minute of it. He was just three semesters from finishing his class work. Then his doctoral dissertation, and he would be Dr. Jeremy Kelly. It had a nice ring to it, Jeremy thought.

"How's the brilliant young professor?" his pretty wife asked him.

"That's graduate assistant. It means I do all the teaching while Dr. Benson gets the credit and the fat paycheck."

They laughed.

"Actually, it wasn't a great day," Jeremy said seriously. He popped a Coke can and stretched out on a kitchen chair. "I had a run-in with Bob Andrews today."

"Bob?" Susan asked with surprise in her voice. "He's your best friend."

"Maybe not anymore, I'm afraid," Jeremy said softly. "I was reviewing his paper on Whitman for him, and came across a section that sounded familiar. It was from a book I'd loaned him last month. He lifted paragraphs out of the book! No quotes. No footnotes. Just word-for-word."

"So what did you do?" Susan sounded concerned.

"I confronted him with it. At first he denied it, but then he knew he was caught. Said that if I told, he'd never talk to me again."

"And . . ."

"I told him he had until tomorrow to make the changes or I'd go to Benson and spill. That kind of stuff isn't right, Susan!" Jeremy sounded angry.

"It'd be easier to let it go and let him take the risk, Jeremy. It's not really your concern." Jeremy leaned closer to his wife. Amanda was playing with his collar button.

"Yeah, well, a long time ago I pulled a dumb stunt like that and I learned a lot when I got caught, Susan. If it weren't for Janet Gill, I might not feel so strongly about this, but ..."

"Who?" Susan was confused.

"Oh, it's not important. I'll tell you the story some day. What's for dinner?"

"Who's cooking?"

Susan and Jeremy laughed and then hugged Amanda between them. Maybe it was a good day, after all.

The End

Jeremy had never been good at lying. His voice always shook.

He worked hard at keeping his voice steady and confident when he told the teacher he didn't know anything about the situation—that he didn't know who the two guys were. It was hard, but Jeremy pulled it off. No one asked him anything else about it.

■

Matt and Justin turned themselves in on Monday morning. They met with their parents and Mrs. Gill at lunch time. Jeremy hung around the office and noticed that when they left, everyone was smiling. Matt and Justin looked at him and gave a "thumbs up" signal on their way out. Jeremy was glad they weren't in deep trouble. He liked the two guys in spite of their craziness, and he knew they liked him too.

■

Chris Miller, Jeremy's biology lab partner, was a lot like Matt and Justin. Cocky, fun and rich. Very rich. Chris' father was an oil company executive, which meant Chris had the latest clothes, more video games than he knew what to do with and a '68 Mustang that every guy and girl on campus envied.

He was one of those kids who tried to buy friendship, and he shopped hard for Jeremy's in the fall. Chris was bright but only at things he liked to do. Somehow, over the years, his money had taught him that if something didn't feel good, he didn't have to taste it, wear it, try it, tolerate it or study it.

"So this fall project is, like, pretty important, is it?" he asked Jeremy as they hung up their lab coats after class.

"Are you kidding? Half your grade hangs on this one, buddy!" Jeremy answered. He couldn't understand how Chris could be so dense so often.

When they got to Jeremy's locker, Chris grabbed his arm and said, "Jeremy, how about we work together on this project? I mean, like partners?"

"Why? You're smart. You can do this stuff in your sleep," Jeremy said, confused.

"No, I've never been good at writing papers. And besides, I've been busy lately. I need some help."

"Busy?" Jeremy laughed. He knew that Chris' idea of busy was a heavy night of MTV.

"Look, Jeremy, I could flunk this course if this project doesn't come out looking good, and you're the one to help me do it. We'll see Mr. Richards tomorrow and get his permission. Then you could do the project."

Jeremy looked up. "I thought you said we'd 'work together' on this thing."

"You know what I mean. I don't know anything about biology. You do the work, I get the credit."

"And what do I get?" Jeremy felt himself getting angry.

"I'll make it worth your while, Jeremy. Name your price. You want to use the Mustang for the homecoming dance? It's yours. Perhaps a hundred bucks would persuade you. Anything!"

Jeremy knew that doing the project was no big deal for him. As a matter of fact, he could probably finish it by the weekend. Biology was easy for Jeremy.

He pushed himself to his feet and looked at Chris.

"I don't know, Chris," he said. "I've got to think about it. I'll get back to you tomorrow. See ya'." And Jeremy walked away.

What would *you* do?

If Jeremy does the project for Chris, turn to page 66.
If he refuses to do it, turn to page 47.

A six-week suspension. The other guys involved got detention for six weeks. But since Jeremy was the main guy, he got the suspension, along with a lecture by Mrs. Gill on responsibility and consequences, and thinking before acting.

All the normal things.

The weeks dragged by. His day began at 8 after Mom and Dad left for work. He'd fix some breakfast, watch game shows and comedy reruns until noon, then walk slowly to the convenience store where Brady and Bruce hung out.

Brady and Bruce Shaw were "world-class drop-outs." That's how they were known at school. Nobody, not even the principal, knew where they were in their education.

Jeremy got lost in the haze of those days. Nothing really seemed to matter. Then the call from the principal brought him back to reality. He was to start school again next Monday. "I'll get your slacks and sport shirts ironed," Mom said, smiling.

Dad seemed pleased too. "Now we can put this behind us, son, and get back to life," he said.

But Jeremy wasn't sure. He liked the drowsy routine he'd developed. And he liked the Shaws. He'd miss them.

Besides, he wasn't sure he could catch up at school. And the six weeks away had changed the way Jeremy looked at himself. His red hair was long and stringy, and he wore grubby clothes almost every day. He found himself unable to look others in the eye, and he was unsure of what to do.

After the clothes had been put out on Sunday night, Mom tossled his hair like she always did and kissed him on the cheek.

"We've got to get you a haircut, young man," she said. "You don't want all your friends at school thinking you're some kind of slob, now, do you?"

How could he tell her? Did he want to go back?

What would *you* do?

If Jeremy says he doesn't want to go back to school, turn to page 53.

If he goes back to school and works hard, turn to page 94.

It hit him while walking through the main library. Jeremy had gone to the library to work on a history report, carrying his papers and note cards in a new backpack his parents had given him. The smell of the library was pleasant, and as he looked up at stacks and stacks of books, it hit him: There was so much to learn in this world. About this world. Why concentrate on learning just to get a well-paying job?

Why not study because . . . well, just because.

So Jeremy picked out a big brown book from a line of books under medieval history, sat at the table and started to read. The chapter was about the feudal system, something he'd never even thought about. Before he knew it, he'd read 52 pages, and it was nearly dinner time. He put the book back on the shelf and left the library feeling great! He hadn't done his assignment, but he had learned.

From that day on, Jeremy vowed he'd study to learn. He'd keep his grades decent, but if a subject interested him, he'd go after it—even if it meant his other grades might hurt a bit.

Teachers like Mr. Mullins inspired Jeremy. Jim Mullins was an older man, 21 years out of college and working at night on a doctorate's degree in history. He had a collection of books that Jeremy used preparing papers and reports. He had an opinion about historical events and didn't just spew facts. Jeremy admired him for that.

"The Protestant Reformation of the 16th century was clearly a politically and economically based revolution," Mr. Mullins said one day as he strode back and forth in front of the class. Jeremy leaned forward to listen.

"Luther was a disturbed—some would even say crazy—monk who established a following among peasants who didn't know better and wealthy landowners who could use him for their personal gain." Mullins leaned against his desk. "What motivated the Reformation was money and power, pure and simple."

"That doesn't sound right." Jeremy spoke out without even raising his hand. Mullins stopped with his mouth open. "Did you say something, Mr. Kelly?" he asked.

"Yes, Mr. Mullins. What about Luther's religious beliefs? his theology? He claimed that people are saved by God's grace alone while the church of that day said they were saved by doing good works. Isn't that the central issue of the Reformation?"

Jim Mullins threw his head back and sighed.

"That theory's been popularized by the church for hundreds of years. But the fact is that if the wealthy landowners didn't see Luther as their champion in order to break with Rome, we'd all be Roman Catholic today. Read your text!"

"I did, and I disagree with that too. Thousands of Christians see it differently . . ."

"Let's keep religion out of this course, Mr. Kelly. I have no use for it. And as long as I'm teaching, it will not be a part of this curriculum. Do you understand?"

The classroom had become quiet. Jeremy was shocked. He'd respected Mr. Mullins for his open mind and his teaching skills, but here there could be no discussion. Jeremy looked around him for some support. Everyone looked down.

What would *you* do?

If Jeremy gets help to confront Mr. Mullins, turn to page 82.
If he drops the subject, turn to page 59.

It sounded corny. And Jeremy would never admit it, but the bright spot in his week was usually Sunday school. It wasn't so much that he was getting deep religious insights every week—he wasn't. But this group of friends was unlike any other, and Beth was good at letting them really discuss things.

"It's dumb to think you're going to learn in high school," Jeremy was saying one Sunday. "I've been in two schools—and both are wastes if you're there to really learn. The bottom line is the GPA. And that's based largely on tests. So ace the tests, and you get into a better school—and you get a better job and make more money."

"And the most important thing is money?" Trish Hughes asked. Her dad was the senior pastor. Jeremy figured she had to talk that way.

"No, Trish. You can live on your winning smile and great personality!" someone else offered. The kids laughed.

Beth leaned forward in her chair. "Jesus did say something about seeking first the things of the kingdom of God, and all the rest will come to you. Seems like we often reverse that."

Jeremy was unimpressed with what seemed like an all-too-simple answer. His life had become complicated. With extra-curricular activities, heavy school work, some great friends and little time for himself, he felt pulled in many different directions. His regular letters to his old friends had stopped, and he found himself being really forgetful. He'd write things on scraps of paper and then forget them. He'd tell his parents he'd run an errand and postpone it until it was too late.

"Keep an appointment book," Mom suggested, "like your father does. It may sound silly, but you've got a lot going on."

So Jeremy did just that. He bought a Day-Timer and wrote in all his appointments, due dates, family activities, church stuff, everything. He used a different color for each area of his life, so his schedule looked like a multicolor spaghetti bowl. But somehow, Jeremy still didn't feel on top of things. He still had too many things to hold onto at once. He knew something was bound to slip through his fingers.

When he walked into algebra class that Monday morning he immediately knew something was wrong. The kids looked strung-out and exhausted as they poured over their texts.

Then it hit! The midterm! He'd spaced the midterm!

The stack of papers on Mr. Wilcox's desk stared him down. He thought of explaining what had happened, but Wilcox would never understand. He'd been prepping the class for this test for two weeks. Jeremy was scared. Algebra was his hardest subject. If he could get a B in this course, that'd help him bring his overall GPA up to the 3.5 level. But the chances of that seemed slim now.

He took his desk and tried a weak smile as Mr. Wilcox placed the paper face down before him. The teacher looked at him with a smile.

"You look relaxed, Jeremy," he said. "Must have this material down, huh?"

"Yeah," Jeremy replied weakly. "No sweat."

Jeremy turned to his right to say hi to Sam, who also had this class, but Sam wasn't there. Instead Tina Ng, the new Vietnamese student, looked back at him from Sam's seat.

Tina noticed his confusion. "Sam is sick," she explained. "Mr. Wilcox told me to sit here." She was quiet, shy and terribly naive, Jeremy thought. And she also kept her paper in full view of Jeremy. As the bell rang, Wilcox gave instructions for the test, and the room fell silent except for the scratching of pencil on paper.

Jeremy looked blankly ahead, but to his right he had a complete view of Tina's paper. And Jeremy wondered what to do.

What would *you* do?

If Jeremy cheats, turn to page 124.
If he doesn't cheat, turn to page 80.

"This locker is starting to look like what's left after a heavy metal concert!" Sam Anderson stood with his hands on his hips, shaking his head. Jeremy stuffed another book into the already-packed locker and leaned against the door until it clicked shut.

The two swung into the flow of hall traffic when suddenly Jeremy was knocked sharply to the side by a rushing body. Mr. Sullivan saw him go down and in his haste yelled back, "Watch where you walk, Kelly. You could hurt somebody!"

"That does it!" Jeremy said as Sam picked him up. "I've put up with him long enough!" And he took off after the mechanics teacher, leaving Sam standing open-mouthed in the hall. Jeremy caught up with Mr. Sullivan as he was unlocking his office door next to the automotive lab.

"Yeah, you want something, Kelly?" Mr. Sullivan asked, turning slightly at the sound of Jeremy approaching.

"Yes, an apology."

Jeremy's words surprised even him. Sullivan turned quickly and looked at him. He spoke angrily, slowly, deliberately. "I beg your pardon."

"That's a start," Jeremy said. "You knocked me down in the hall, and you didn't even say 'I'm sorry.' That's rude, Mr. Sullivan, and I don't care if you *are* a teacher. You still owe me an apology."

Sullivan stood staring at Jeremy for what seemed forever. Then he opened the door and motioned Jeremy inside. The two sat in silence for a long minute, and then the teacher said softly, "I'm sorry."

More silence. Jeremy didn't say a word. He was taken back and actually felt foolish for making such a big deal out of the incident.

"It's okay, Mr. Sullivan. You were in a hurry, and I guess you didn't think to ..." Mr. Sullivan raised a big, calloused hand, cutting off Jeremy's sentence.

"No, that's the problem. I'm not very good at being courteous to kids anymore. Guess it comes with getting old. I was never that way years ago. I actually enjoyed teaching—enjoyed kids. But I've been at this now for 21 years, and it seems every day I get a little angrier. And I take it out on you guys. Please forgive me."

Jeremy held out his hand, and the shop teacher shook it firmly.

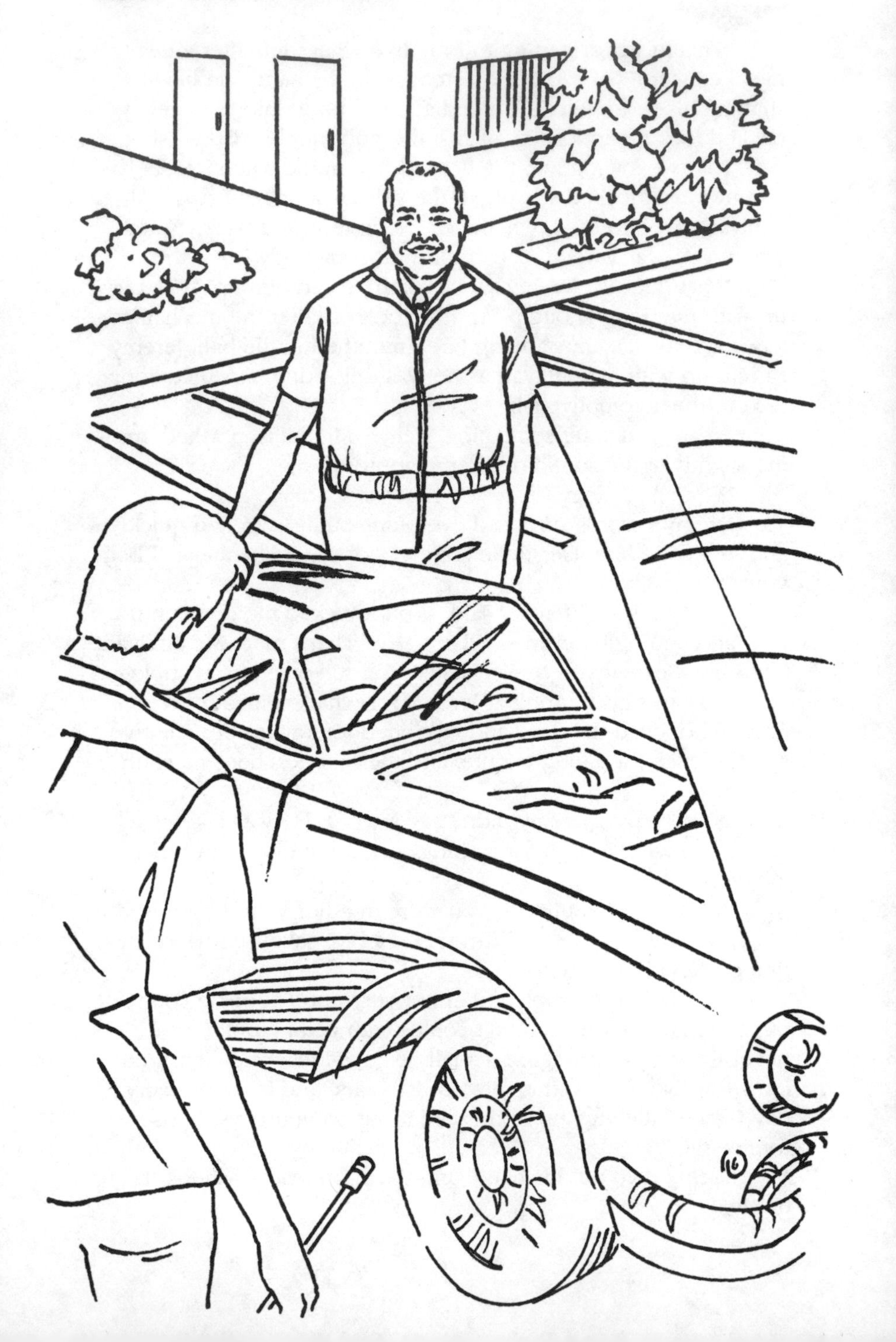

■

Mr. Sullivan actually seemed to mellow after that. He invited Jeremy to come in after school and work with him tuning up his old Corvette. Jeremy respected him and was learning far more than he would from any book.

■

"So how goes the teacher's favorite mechanic?" Gary Carlsen looked up from his text as Jeremy sat down in mechanics class one Thursday.

Randy Adams laughed. "You been putting in the hours to get that grade up, haven't you, Kelly?" Randy snickered. "That's one way to graduate on top."

They both laughed. "Sullivan's a good guy," Jeremy cut in, "and he likes my work. Why don't you guys stop by after school?"

But the two laughed and turned away.

■

"I'd say they're jealous," Beth told Jeremy before youth group that Sunday.

"Maybe I should quit working with him after school. If the kids think I'm after grades . . . "

"Do you want to stop working with him?" Beth asked.

"No."

"Do you think God wants you to stop working with him?" she asked.

"No, I don't think so. But I haven't really prayed about it much."

"Maybe that's where you should start, then," Beth said. "Find out what God wants you to do, then do it. You can never go wrong by following his guidance."

"Good idea, Beth," Jeremy said. "I just hope God can get through to me."

What would *you* do?

If Jeremy ignores the kids and keeps working with Mr. Sullivan, turn to page 10.
If he stops working with Mr. Sullivan, turn to page 96.

Red tape.

From one meeting with Mr. Johnson to another with Mrs. Gill. Then three pages of forms to complete, followed by a long meeting with the facilities board and a longer wait until lawyers could be consulted.

Finally a note:

"A Bible study on school grounds is permissible provided that:

1. It's student-led;
2. It isn't advertised as an official school function; and
3. No student is excluded from the Bible study on the basis of religious preference or any other criteria."

The note went on to say they could hold the Bible study in Room 224 on Wednesday mornings between 7 and 7:45.

The little classroom was packed for the first Bible study. Craig Morris was there with a huge Bible in a leather case. Mark Sims, Jake Ward, Sam Anderson and Trish Hughes were there from church. At 7 sharp, Jeremy shouted over the noise, "Hey, you guys, let's study the Bible!" And the room grew quiet.

"Uh, let's pray," he said and then bowed his head.

"Dear God, bless this Bible study and bless our school. Help us learn more about you from your Word, and help us learn to love people more so we stop putting them down. In Jesus' name, amen."

And the whole room said, "Amen."

Blind choice:

Without looking ahead, turn to page 34 or page 36 to see how the Bible study turns out.

After school that day, Jeremy was walking toward the field house when he heard the sound of rubber slapping the pavement. He turned to see Chris running toward him. Jeremy stopped and turned.

"You got me in deep trouble, Kelly!" Chris' face was red, and Jeremy didn't know if he'd have to fight or not. But Chris just stood there, fists clenched, looking awkward.

"Stop blaming everyone else for your problems, Miller!" Jeremy felt himself getting angry. He knew he could handle Chris if he had to, but it would be dumb to fight.

"You're my problem, Kelly!"

"Me? I'm not your problem. I've done you a favor!" Jeremy yelled.

"Yeah? How?" Chris looked furious.

Jeremy composed himself. "Friends don't cheat for other friends, Chris." Chris took a deep breath. Then Jeremy continued. "Friends, real friends, tell the truth. And the truth is you'll graduate from this place in two years not knowing a thing except how to con a teacher. You're smarter than that."

There was a long silence. Jeremy knew he'd struck a nerve. Finally Chris spoke.

"You're right. I'm wearing myself out cheating. It might be easier just to do the work. But I don't know how."

"I'll teach you. It's not hard to study once you know some basic rules. Why not come over tonight?"

■

Chris was early for their 6:30 study session that night. He looked strange with a pile of books under his arm, but he also looked like he was about to begin a new adventure. By the end of the night he'd actually completed a chapter in his biology book and held up his answer sheet like an athlete holding a trophy.

"Would you believe?" Chris asked proudly. "This is the first biology assignment I've completed this year. And I've been getting a C average!"

"So how does it feel?" Jeremy felt like a proud teacher.

"Great. And I actually understand cell structure. You're a good teacher, Kelly."

The two met throughout the week and into the next. Chris' grades continued to improve and so did the guys' friendship. One afternoon as they studied together in the library, Chris pointed to a young man standing by the American literature stacks.

"Well, look who's here," he said softly with a lisp in his voice.

"Yeah, that's Mr. Newton, the new English teacher." Jeremy looked back down at his assignment sheet.

"You know he's, uh," Chris paused and Jeremy looked up. Chris continued, "he's a fag."

"Excuse me?" Jeremy put his pen on the table. The librarian was looking at them.

Chris was whispering. "He's gay. All the guys say so. You can tell just by looking at him. And when you listen to him talk, it's kind of like girls talk. You know."

Jeremy looked over at the slight young man with the full head of blond, curly hair. He knew that Carl Newton was just out of college, that he lived with a group of guys in a house downtown and that he loved to jog. Kids in his classes already said he was one of the most fun English teachers at Windy Point.

Carl Newton took some books from the shelf and walked toward them. He smiled and said, "Hi, guys!" When he had passed, Chris puckered his lips, made a limp gesture with his hand and covered his laughter.

Jeremy was silent. Mr. Newton? Gay? Was it true or just an unfounded rumor?

What would *you* do?

If Jeremy believes the rumor, turn to page 44.
If he rejects the rumor, turn to page 85.

Jeremy jumped from the bus the next day to see Justin, Matt and two other guys roar out of the south parking lot on their way to a day of four-wheeling. Oh well, it isn't worth the risk, Jeremy figured. But it would've been fun. He didn't care much about school, but he didn't want to risk detention either.

He explained his logic to some kids at lunch later, and their reactions surprised him.

"You're too easy-going, Jeremy," Trish Hughes scolded. "I mean, you've got to work hard if you want to get into a good college after you graduate."

"I guess pastors' kids get into preaching too, right Trish?" Jeremy joked, and the kids laughed.

"No, Trish is right," Craig Morris said. "This is a really competitive school, and if you don't do your best here, you can forget about getting into a good college. That's just the way it is."

"So why would you want to get into a good college?" Jeremy knew he was starting an argument, but he wanted to talk this out.

"Simple. So you can get a good job and earn lots of money." Craig spoke with authority. Like it had to be right.

"Not necessarily," Trish said. "I just enjoy studying. I like learning things. Answering questions so that more questions are raised. I plan to get a liberal-arts degree in college and not worry about a job. That'll come in time."

"You can't live on questions, Trish." Craig loved to pick on Trish, but she didn't budge.

"God gives us a great world, and I'm going to find out as much about it as I can. I think learning is exciting!"

Jeremy admired Trish for feeling that way, but he could also see Craig's point. Jeremy wanted to make money and live comfortably when he got older. But he was curious about a lot of things.

Should he learn in order to gain security and money? Or should learning be a goal in itself, just because it's important? Jeremy knew his answer to those questions would shape his attitude toward school. He really wasn't sure.

What would *you* do?

If Jeremy studies to get a good job and money, turn to page 105.
If he studies for the sake of learning, turn to page 103.

Jeremy planned his exit well.

He stayed upstairs, listening for his parents' movements. When he heard the downstairs bedroom door close, he slipped down stairs and dashed out the door to the bus stop. Sam Anderson and Craig Morris, two of Jeremy's new friends, were watching from the bus as it waited for him. He hopped on and the bus pulled away.

"You were moving, man!" Sam said. "Why such a rush?"

"My parents have been hassling me," Jeremy grunted. "They want me to rework my class schedule to make it harder. I didn't want to talk to them."

"So what happens if you don't do it?" Craig asked.

"No hoops," Jeremy looked out the window. "Big deal."

By 1:30 that afternoon Jeremy was totally bored. English basics used the same text he'd used in a class in Chicago. And in health and fitness, he watched a video on tooth decay. By the time he sat down in his last class, Jeremy was a brainless zombie.

"Hey, Kelly." Jeremy heard a whisper coming from across the aisle. "You want to have a little fun tomorrow?" It was Matt Brondos, a guy Jeremy had talked to a few times.

"Huh?" Jeremy blinked hard to wake himself up.

"We're going to do a little four-wheeling tomorrow. Want to come along?" Matt's whisper was getting a little louder.

"What do you mean?" Jeremy asked, leaning across the aisle. "We've got school all day."

Justin Parsons, in front of him, nearly laughed out loud.

"Kelly, you're so naive!" Justin was turning all the way around. "The city's having a flu epidemic. It's been hitting people for two weeks now. Some of us plan to become very ill." Justin and Matt laughed, and the teacher looked up as she prepared her notes.

All these courses are a waste! Jeremy thought. But it's only the first day of school. It could get better. Why not give it a chance?

"So what d'ya say, Jeremy?" Justin was leaning back in his chair. "We gonna see you tomorrow?"

What would *you* do?

If Jeremy skips school and goes four-wheeling, turn to page 25.
If he stays in school, turn to page 113.

Jeremy pulled off his headphones and fumbled through the cards. After almost dropping everything on the floor, he handed the teacher a stack of cards.

Mr. Richards looked up and smiled. "Pretty hard stuff, uh ... Jeremy. You've got your hands full here. Can you do it?"

"Sure, no sweat," he said. What have I done? he thought.

But Jeremy felt he had to prove himself somehow. In his mind, he heard Ben and Kenny behind him, letting him know what they thought of wimps, especially kids who take the easy way out. He thought of college in three years and knew how much it'd mean to his folks for him to approach school seriously.

Besides, there was an attitude here. Only the best clothes, the latest hair styles. These guys *looked* expensive, and they acted the part too—really competitive. It wasn't like his old school where everyone was more laid-back and accepting. Here, in the new school, every decimal point on your grade mattered.

Mr. Richards handed Jeremy a printout of the classes he'd chosen.

"Okay, Jeremy, you've signed up for world history, algebra, biology, English literature, Spanish, and Earth sciences. Please sign at the bottom here."

Jeremy picked up the pen next to the printout. Well, there goes my life for the next four months, he thought.

And he signed the form.

■

"You've really taken on a heavy load, Jeremy," his father commented at dinner that evening. "I hope you can still get some time in for sports and church activities. We hear the youth group at church is great."

"Why *did* you decide on these courses, Son?" his mother asked as she handed him the salad. "It seems awfully ambitious."

"Nah," Jeremy mumbled. "It's not all that bad. I figure ... it's like a whole new start. And maybe I should push myself a little."

"Well, if you put your mind to it, I'm sure you can do it," Dad said, adjusting his glasses.

"That may be true, Bill," Mom turned to Dad, "but I just hope he's doing it for the right reasons. That's a lot of work for a 15-year-old."

"He's a big boy now," Dad answered. "It's his first semester in a new school, and he knows what he can handle."

"Ah, excuse me," Jeremy said with a smile. "Can I get into this conversation? Mom, don't you think I can do it?"

"That's not the point, Jeremy," Dad said. "Your mother knows you can do the work if you want to, but I think she's concerned about your reasons for taking on a heavy load."

"Are you doing this to prove yourself to these new kids?" Mom asked.

"No," Jeremy said, rolling his eyes.

"Well, something must've influenced you to do this," Mom responded. "Either it's these new kids or pressure about college or . . . Jeremy, do you think you have to prove yourself to us?"

"C'mon, Mom," Jeremy was getting angry now. "Give me a break, okay? I just wanted to, that's all."

Dad looked straight at him now.

"Jeremy, I think you should figure out what motivated you to sign up for these courses. You need to be honest with yourself—and with us."

What would *you* do?

If Jeremy is doing it for his parents, turn to page 70.
If he is doing it for himself, turn to page 131.
If he is doing it to prove himself in the new school, turn to page 28.

"Do you remember . . . ?"

It seemed every sentence began with those words. The room was filled with his old college friends, and the hugging and joking were making this a night to remember. It was the five-year reunion of Jeremy's college class.

Jeremy had graduated from Gundermann five years ago. He wasn't at the top of his class, but he was able to get into graduate school and complete a master's degree in education. He'd chosen secondary education and had come back to the high school that had given him so much.

Jeremy loved Windy Point High School, but he'd been afraid he'd have a hard time working with people who'd been his teachers. Still, it seemed worth it. He was in his second year on the student-counseling staff.

"Weird—that's what it is," Jeremy was saying to Melanie Anderson and Bill Percy, two old college friends. "I was planning to go into the Peace Corps for a few years, but then Mom calls and says they're looking for a student counselor at my old high school. So I applied and got the job."

"Do you have a hard time fitting in with the faculty?" Melanie asked.

Jeremy laughed. "They respect me, but Mr. Johnson, er, Alex, loves to remind me of my struggles." Jeremy paused and laughed to himself as he remembered his high school days. "Anyway," he continued, "it wasn't easy, and sometimes I don't know how I made it as far as I did."

"Nobody warned us about the decisions we'd have to make," Melanie said.

Bill agreed. "And each one had its own set of consequences."

Jeremy was thoughtful. "I heard an old saying once," he said. " 'Everyone has the right to choose, but you can't choose the consequences of what you choose.' That's the story of my high school years!"

His two friends agreed.

"It turned out okay, Jeremy," Melanie said. "We're doing what we want to do, and maybe you can even help kids make good decisions."

Jeremy smiled. "I hope so. If they only knew the crazy things we did. Oh, the stories we could tell!"

The End

Jeremy didn't take much time to pray about his decision. It seemed clear to him that God would provide a college for him if he was supposed to go.

So Jeremy let Mr. Campbell know of his decision not to attend summer school. Instead, he worked at Fisher Automotive.

■

College seemed so far away then, but the next school year was flying by. And soon choices about colleges had to be made.

Catalogs were scattered over the floor of his bedroom, and Jeremy arranged them into three neat piles: "Best," "Good" and "If I have to."

Around Christmas of his senior year, Jeremy sent out applications. Responses started arriving in February.

"Thank you for your application. We regret to inform you ..."

"Your grades and selection of courses do not warrant ..."

"Additional courses in the areas of math and science would be necessary ..."

Jeremy threw the letters on his bed and walked to his desk. These guys know more ways to say no, he thought.

Mr. Campbell was right. If he'd taken those summer-school courses, his chances of getting into the good schools might be better. But who could say?

It had been a good summer. He still worked part time at Fisher Automotive, and there were two more colleges left to respond.

Anderson State College's letter was brief and to the point. "We cannot accept you at this time." Finally, a college that said what they meant, Jeremy thought.

But Metropolitan Community College had a letter that sounded more like "Sure, why not?"

And so, in the fall following graduation, Jeremy started classes at Metropolitan Community College. It wasn't a bad school, and he could probably transfer to another college after two years. Only when his friends were home from college for vacations—talking about fraternity life and the excitement of other parts of the country—did Jeremy have some regrets.

He *had* enjoyed working at Fisher Automotive.

The End

It was a dumb thing to do. Jeremy knew that, and the time spent working around the school after classes only made him realize it all the more. He had the job of picking up trash in the parking lots for an hour and a half after classes. He was starting to dream about the soft drink cans, candy wrappers and cigarette butts each night.

The kids gave him a hard time during the first week, but soon they left him alone. He'd police the parking lots, thinking about why he was there and what he could do to change.

Twice a week Jeremy met with Anita Mendoza, a counselor who worked for the school district. Short and pretty with long dark hair, Anita listened to Jeremy like he was the most important person on Earth, and her questions made him think about things he'd never taken seriously before.

"I don't know why I do dumb things like that," Jeremy was saying one Wednesday afternoon. "I never thought it'd get me in this much trouble. I always thought it wouldn't matter."

"Like you could do whatever you wanted, and there'd be no consequences," Anita said.

"Yeah, like I don't matter to anyone," Jeremy said. "Maybe that's it. Maybe it's like I could do whatever I wanted, and it wouldn't matter." Jeremy slumped deeper into his chair and frowned.

"Jeremy, that's what children believe. That they can do anything they want, and it won't matter. But when we grow up, we begin to understand that our actions are important and have consequences. And that's why you're here."

When Anita said things like that, Jeremy half-believed them. She didn't sound like his mother lecturing on "responsibility." Anita seemed to take him seriously as an adult, and that felt good to him. It was also scary for Jeremy—to see himself as an adult.

Beth Faulkes, the youth minister at church, was helpful too. One day she pulled her little red Volkswagen Beetle into the parking lot as Jeremy was finishing his clean-up and tossed a crushed Coke can in front of him.

"Hey, shorty, you forgot one," she teased. Jeremy shook his head and threw the can into the plastic sack.

"You ready to get out of detention and get back to your regular classes?" It was clear that Beth wanted to hear a yes.

"I don't know. I really don't," Jeremy said, dropping to the grass. Beth sat beside him, looking puzzled.

"It's not that I don't want to get this behind me. I'm just not sure I can make it," Jeremy said. "I really messed up bad, and, well, maybe it's just the way I am. Maybe I can't handle the pressures of school."

"Look, Jeremy, 'forgiveness' means you wipe the board clean and start all over again. That's what you've got to do. You can't forget what you did. It was wrong. But you can accept God's forgiveness and forgive yourself."

Jeremy pushed himself to his feet and picked up the plastic sack.

"I know. I just wish it was that easy. Detention's over on Friday, and Mrs. Gill will want to know how my attitude has changed. I'm still not sure what to tell her. Part of me wants to dig right into school. The other part wants to quit school, take a job and make life a lot easier."

"C'mon, Jeremy, you're better than that. Stick with it." Beth spoke with emotion. "We'll hang in there with you, and you'll make it. You can do it!" She gave Jeremy a hug and jumped in her car.

"Let me know what you decide, okay?"

Jeremy nodded.

What would *you* do?

If Jeremy gets serious about school, turn to page 94.
If he drops out, turn to page 53.

Jeremy's basketball locker was twice the size of his hall unit, but it seemed just as full. Jeremy pulled out smelly, sweaty clothes, two pairs of high-tops, play books, candy wrappers and water bottles. He sorted through the stuff, which he either threw away or crammed into a canvas gym bag.

Jeremy would miss basketball, but school was more important. He couldn't keep the routine required for basketball and watch his grades drop. Something had to go. College was too important to Jeremy to sacrifice it. And Jeremy felt this was what God wanted him to do.

■

"I'm not sure you can get those grades up with the time remaining, Jeremy," Mr. Campbell, his grade adviser, told Jeremy the next day. "At this point, you're likely to get D's in three of your six courses. You're running a low C in algebra and an F in biology. This is sure turning out to be a rough semester for you, Jeremy."

"Yeah, but you should see my jump shot," Jeremy said with a smile. It wasn't funny.

"What can I do, Mr. Campbell?" Jeremy asked. "I really want to get into a good college. I know I have two more years, but I don't want to start off this bad."

"Well, there's always summer school, Jeremy. It would mean quite a commitment on your part. You could take algebra and biology over, and maybe a few other courses to boost your grade point for next year."

"What a wonderful way to spend a summer," he said sarcastically.

"True, but it would ease your course load next year, and some good grades would look good on this transcript."

Jeremy thanked Mr. Campbell and walked out into the sunshine. It was a beautiful spring day—warm and dry without a cloud in the sky.

Lord, where are you? Jeremy yelled in his mind. What am I supposed to do now? I need you to help me make a decision.

What would *you* do?

If Jeremy goes to summer school, turn to page 57.
If he decides against summer school, turn to page 118.

Mom and Dad were already settled in the living room when Jeremy asked if he could talk with them for a minute.

Jeremy was nervous as he spoke. "Mom, during dinner you asked about the SAT exam." His mother nodded.

"I'm not going to be taking the SAT. I don't want to go to college."

Dad dropped the newspaper to his lap. Mom sat motionless.

"No college? Why, Son?" Dad sounded disappointed, and Jeremy felt terrible. He didn't want to hurt his parents.

"It's just that I'm not college material, Dad. I don't like studying all that much, and the idea of four more years of exams and papers and reading really turns me off. I just can't do it."

Dad was annoyed. "Now, Jeremy, you know that kids who don't go to college earn much less than those who do, and your mother and I have . . . "

"Bill," Mom put her hand on Dad's arm. "Let him talk."

Jeremy continued. "I don't want to hurt you, and I know you expected me to go right from high school to college, but there are other good options. Maybe I'll join the Army or go to trade school. Anything but college!"

Dad thought for a moment, then shook his head.

"For so many years, I've imagined you on some college campus. I guess I never imagined you wouldn't want to go. But you're old enough to make your own decisions."

"You do what you think is right, Son" Mom said.

Jeremy was so happy he wanted to cry. For the first time in a long time he felt really free. He could stop pretending he wanted to be "Joe College" and get on with being Jeremy Kelly.

■

Jeremy's graduation party was great! The house was packed with friends from church and school, and right in the middle of it all, his parents took him aside and gave him a package. It contained a wrist watch inscribed with the date and "To Our Jeremy—We're So Proud of You! Love, Mom and Dad."

"The inscription's the greatest gift," Jeremy said as he hugged them. "To know that you're proud of me no matter what I decide. That's what love is all about!"

The End

It wasn't as though Jeremy didn't know the material. He'd just neglected to study it. He just had to get himself organized. It wasn't like he did this all the time. Matter of fact, he'd never "borrowed information" before in his life. This was the first time, and, Jeremy vowed, it'd be the last.

Distracting thoughts kept going through his mind as his eyes glanced across the aisle at Tina's paper. Thoughts that told him he shouldn't be doing this, that it was wrong. Thoughts he ignored.

Tina kept her head down and Jeremy lowered his head just far enough so he could see her paper. He wrote fast. The first section was multiple choice, and Jeremy was able to get about half of them from his memory. Tina's paper helped with the rest.

Her formulas and figures were large and clear, something that surprised Jeremy. He filled in the formulas on the test, and as he did, he realized it really made sense. Tina was right. She really knew her algebra and was going for an A. And Jeremy with her.

It isn't that I don't know it, he kept thinking. I just don't have time to study it. I'm serving my school. I'm becoming more well-rounded than some of these guys. That's important too. Jeremy realized that his mind was wandering from the test, and he covered his eyes with his hand as he stole another glance at Tina's paper. Page 4. The last page.

"Mr. Kelly, may I see you?" The teacher's deep voice boomed through the silence of the classroom. Jeremy felt the hairs on his arms go straight. He shivered in the heat of the classroom.

"Me, sir?" his voice quivered.

"You are Mr. Kelly, are you not, Jeremy?" Mr. Wilcox's voice was deeper, more stern now. Others in the classroom were looking at him. Tina moved her paper farther to the right and leaned down to cover it with her shoulder as if she knew.

"Uh, sure," Jeremy said. He turned his paper over on his desk and pushed himself out of his seat. His knees were so weak, he wasn't sure he could make the walk up to the desk. Mr. Wilcox sat facing him like a judge in a courtroom.

Blind choice:

Without looking ahead, turn to page 8 or page 74 to see what happens to Jeremy.

Alan Richards looked up at the two in a silence that seemed to last forever.

"Guys, I've been a teacher for a long time, and you begin to notice things after a while. Like how kids sit in class and how test papers look alike."

Jeremy felt his stomach growing sick. Mr. Richards continued.

"It's when answers look the same that you get suspicious." He put the two test papers side by side on the desk in front of him. Jeremy noticed that Chris was sweating heavily.

"But when words get misspelled in the same way—that's the tip-off."

Alan pointed to the word "nucleus" that both boys had spelled with an "i" where the "e" should've been. Dumb.

"You want to tell me about it?" Alan asked them.

"A coincidence?" Chris said softly.

"Doubt it. Jeremy, what do you say for yourself?"

"Yeah, we cheated," Jeremy said. Chris looked at him amazed.

"Then let's take a walk to the principal's office," Alan said, pushing his chair away from the desk.

■

The students at Windy Point High School liked Janet Gill. She looked small and efficient as she stood over Chris and Jeremy in her office. The boys felt cramped on the small couch, and Mrs. Gill walked back and forth several times before speaking.

"Chris Miller, this is the second time you've been in here for cheating, isn't it?"

"Yeah," Chris said softly. Jeremy knew it meant nothing to Chris.

"I've called your parents, and they'll be here later this afternoon for a meeting. I'm recommending suspension and counseling for you, Chris. You've got an attitude to take care of." Mrs. Gill's voice sounded angry and compassionate at the same time, Jeremy thought. She dismissed Chris.

After Chris left, Mrs. Gill glanced in a Manila folder, then turned to look at Jeremy. "As for you, Jeremy, there are no bad reports in your file since you started here. What's happening now?" She sat down in a chair next to him.

"I guess I let myself get talked into things that aren't good for me," Jeremy said, looking directly at her. "I felt sorry for Chris, so I let him cheat off my paper."

"You know why that's wrong?" It was a question and a statement in one.

"Yeah. It doesn't help Chris, and it gets me in trouble."

"No, there's more than that, Jeremy," Mrs. Gill said seriously. "Nobody can do your education for you. It's the most precious thing you've got, and when you treat it like some stuff to throw around," her voice sounded sarcastic, "you cheapen yourself and your knowledge. Understand?"

Jeremy nodded. He thought he understood.

Mrs. Gill got up and walked to the desk. She picked up the file folder.

"Look, this is your first time and I hope it's your last. I hope you've learned your lesson. I'm not taking any disciplinary action. Do you think you can change?"

Jeremy was shocked! Nothing! "Yeah, of course," he said with obvious surprise in his voice. "You bet!"

"Then, you can go, Jeremy. I hope the next time we meet it'll be under more pleasant conditions."

Jeremy closed the principal's door behind him as he walked to his locker. No discipline. Could he change? Yeah, sure, he thought to himself. Why not?

What would *you* do?

If Jeremy changes, turn to page 98.
If he doesn't change, turn to page 33.

"Well, if they don't like me, it's their loss."

Jeremy tried to sound cool, but as he looked at himself in the locker mirror, he knew the jocks were right.

Geek.

It wasn't as though he'd set out to be a geek. He didn't check any kind of "geek manual" or anything like that. He was just too busy. But he didn't like the results of his negligence.

"Some things will have to change," Jeremy muttered to himself as he slammed the door and clicked the lock. "No more geek."

It was a Friday afternoon, and he talked his mom into giving him the clothes money she'd set aside in late August. It just hadn't seemed important to him until now.

Saturday, he got a haircut at Shear Delights. Then spent the rest of the day buying new clothes.

By Monday morning, he'd lost the geek look.

Jeremy couldn't believe how many people stopped by his locker as he got his books for first hour.

"Hey, cool! The new Jeremy Kelly!"

"Whooowie—Kelly, you're stylin'."

Jeremy soon noticed that the "new look" opened up new friendships. The jocks liked Jeremy's sense of humor. And Chris Miller, Jeremy's rich biology lab partner, was now talking with him. Jeremy had even gone out with Chris and his friends one Friday night.

After biology class one day, Chris grabbed Jeremy by the arm as the crowd of kids pushed for the door.

"Hey, Jeremy, got a minute?"

Jeremy nodded. And Chris pulled him off into a corner and leaned close.

"I'm in a bit of a jam with this course," Chris said.

Jeremy knew that. Chris didn't study. He spent too much time cruising, dating and watching MTV.

"I've got to get a good grade on the exam tomorrow," Chris said with worry in his voice. "If I don't, I could blow the class."

"So? How can I help you?" Jeremy was getting a little annoyed.

"I'd like to, you know, be able to, uh, share your answers."

"Share my answers?" Jeremy laughed so loud kids turned to look.

"Look, Jeremy, just because you've got some new clothes doesn't mean you're cool." Chris' voice turned harsh. "You're going to need some friends—maybe a hot car to borrow once in a while. And I can make those things happen. Like the song says, 'That's what friends are for.' "

Jeremy stood up straight and looked up at Chris.

"And what if friends don't help other friends cheat?"

"Then they aren't friends." Chris' voice was cold.

Jeremy looked down for a moment. "I'll think about it. See ya' tomorrow."

And he walked away.

What would *you* do?

If Jeremy lets Chris cheat, turn to page 27.

If he refuses to let him cheat, turn to page 87.

Alan Richards, Jeremy's biology teacher, put the test face down in front of Jeremy, and Jeremy drummed his fingers on it for a moment before turning it over. He automatically broke into a grin. An 89! With the curve it translated into an A! Jeremy couldn't believe it!

Not that he thought he'd flunked. He knew he did well—but not this well.

Jeremy noticed Chris Miller leaning over, looking at Jeremy's score. The red F branded the top of Chris' page. Next to it, in the same searing red, Mr. Richards wrote, "See me!"

"Hey, sorry about that," Jeremy said to Chris.

"Yeah. Congratulations," Chris nodded.

The next few weeks went well for Jeremy. He was in a study routine—three hours of homework between the end of classes and free time. In his mind he treated study like a part-time job, and it was paying off. So well, in fact, that Jeremy even considered going out for basketball.

"I'm beginning to feel like Wally Cleaver," he said to Chris as they walked out of biology one day.

"Hey, lucky you," Chris said as Jeremy walked up to his locker.

"Still having trouble with biology?" Jeremy asked.

"Yeah." Chris kicked the bottom of the locker as he spoke. "I just can't seem to get my act together, you know?"

Jeremy smiled. He knew Chris could get the same grades as he did, but Chris was lazy. He liked driving his classic Mustang after school, and spent most nights in front of the television. Chris' parents traveled a lot, and they didn't encourage him much.

"Jeremy, I've got this problem," Chris said as they walked down the hall. "My biology project is really bugging me." The project counted for one-fourth of the final grade. "I need help," Chris said.

Jeremy stopped. "What do you mean?" he asked.

Chris grinned. "Here's my idea: We'll tell Richards we want to double up on the project. You know, we'll do the research together, and it'll be twice as big as a regular project."

"That's a neat idea, Chris," Jeremy said, seeing an opportunity to make a friend. "I can help you catch up on some of the work too."

"No, you don't understand, buddy." Chris smiled. "I'll let you do the work. I don't understand this stuff anyway, and you're good. You can do this stuff in your sleep. I just want half the credit."

"Sounds like a one-sided deal to me," Jeremy said, not sure whether Chris was serious.

"I'll make it worth your while, Jeremy. Just name your price. You want to use my Mustang for the homecoming dance? It's yours. You need some money? Perhaps a hundred bucks would persuade you."

Jeremy stood silent for a second. Then he said, "I'll have to let you know tomorrow, Chris. Okay?"

"Yeah, sure," Chris chuckled. "Tomorrow."

It's going to be a long night, Jeremy thought as he walked to his next class.

What would *you* do?

If Jeremy does the project for Chris, turn to page 66.
If he refuses to share the project, turn to page 47.

Jeremy never answered his parents' questions that night. But in his own mind he'd come to a conclusion: School was his personal proving ground. If he could succeed in school, he could succeed anywhere. And if he didn't, he'd be a first-rate failure. So he needed to tackle a heavy class load to prove to himself he could do it.

■

"Hey, hermit, how about some one-on-one in the driveway?" Two weeks had passed, and Jeremy's dad was standing under Jeremy's window bouncing a basketball on the concrete driveway. It was about 6 p.m.

"Not now, Dad. I've got four chapters of *King Lear*, and another hour of algebra." Jeremy had been studying since 4:30, and his eyes felt like they were going to drop out of their sockets. The course load was wearing him down, but he loved it! He'd discovered that learning can be fun.

From the moment he rolled out of bed in the morning until he turned off the light at night, he studied. He'd read on the school bus, and on Sundays he'd stick a paperback in his pocket just in case he had a few minutes at church.

It was never like this back in Chicago. Never the excitement of learning. The teachers at Windy Point High School loved their subjects, and they passed their love on to the kids.

"If only Ben and Kenny could see me now!" Jeremy laughed as he left for school the next Monday. They used to go together to men's stores in the mall, and try to find "cool" clothes they could afford.

Now, Jeremy had to be reminded to brush his teeth in the morning. He'd skip a shower to read a few extra pages, and his greasy hair lay matted over his right ear. Same old flannel shirt and jeans each day. And when his mother would scold him, he'd say something about "more important things than looking cool."

It was the first day of semester exams. The noise level in the hall was insane, and elbows were everywhere.

Jeremy sat in the middle of a packed room in front of two cheerleaders in their uniforms and two muscular football players in their letter jackets.

The tall guy looks like Kenny, Jeremy thought. For a minute he felt a little homesick.

"Oh, how swell," the tall, jock behind him said to the cheerleader across the aisle. "We've got a geek life-form in front of us. Maybe the brain power will rub off on us poor, dumb jocks."

It took Jeremy a moment to realize they were talking about him.

Geek. It was a cruel word, one that he and Ben and Kenny had used about a lot of the quiet, studious types in their old school. They threw it out and blew it off. But now it was directed at him: geek.

He ran his hand over his greasy hair. He'd been up most of the night studying. Hadn't had a chance to shampoo or blow it out. It felt long and stringy.

Jeremy looked down at his shirt. Four pencils and pens in the pocket of an old flannel shirt that stuck half-in, half-out of his jeans. No socks in his running shoes. He just . . . forgot.

Geek.

The papers were being passed out, and the teacher was explaining test rules. But Jeremy wasn't listening. Only one word was in his mind.

Geek.

Could that be me? he pondered. I love to study. I love this stuff. But does that mean I've become my own worst nightmare? Geek!

What would *you* do?

If Jeremy ignores the comment, turn to page 49.
If he tries to change his image, turn to page 127.